ORDINARY
MAGIC

Also by Malcolm Bosse

The Vast Memory of Love
Mister Touch
Stranger at the Gate
Fire in Heaven
The Warlord
The Man Who Loved Zoos
The Incident at Naha
The Journey of Tao Kim Nam

For Young Adults
Deep Dream of the Rain Forest
Captives of Time
The Barracuda Gang
Cave Beyond Time
The 79 Squares

ORDINARY MAGIC

Malcolm Bosse

A Sunburst Book   Farrar, Straus and Giroux

To C. G. Vasudevan
My student, my teacher, my friend—
Om Sri Ganeshaya Namah

The author wishes to thank the National Endowment for the Arts for helping to make this book possible.

Library of Congress catalog card number: 93-7956
First published in the United States by Thomas Y. Crowell
under the title *Ganesh*
Published in Canada by HarperCollins*CanadaLtd*
Printed in the United States of America
First edition, 1981
Sunburst edition, 1993
Second printing, 1996

ORDINARY MAGIC

Part I

Stopping outside the Mission School grounds, he wrapped a long piece of cloth in a turban's shape around his blond head. Although Jeffrey had lived all of his fourteen years in India, his fair skin was still vulnerable to the Indian sun. Without something covering his head, he could easily get sunstroke. In the hot season everyone he saw had some kind of protection: a turban, an umbrella, a handkerchief, even a newspaper draped over the head.

The Mission School was a few kilometers from his village, so Jeffrey headed down the paved road, swinging from his shoulder a packet of books secured with an old belt. Heat waves were snaking up from the macadam into the sunlight, causing his light blue eyes to squint in the glare. Even in sandals the soles of his feet became so hot that soon he had to stop and cool off. He stood under a scarred old banyan tree, near a flock of white egrets who posed motionlessly at the edge of a paddy. They would not approach the rice shoots, even though hungry for the ripening kernels, because a tattered scarecrow kept watch in the middle of the field. Jeffrey leaned for a few minutes against the tree trunk and stared at a sluggish stream that ran parallel to the road; the water was polka-dotted with lotus buds ready to burst into white and purple blossoms, like a liquid orchard under the blaze of summer. Adjusting the turban, he then proceeded into the outskirts of his village.

Plaster-and-thatch huts lined the way; inside their dark interiors men sipped tea or repaired bicycles or sold turmeric powder. At one entrance four men played cards on a bamboo mat, while behind them a radio was blaring film music. One of the men, smiling, waved at Jeffrey, who waved back. "Do you ever open those books, Ganesh?" the man asked with a grin. Ganesh was Jeffrey's nickname. "Play," another man said irritably and threw down a card. They spoke in Tamil, a language that Jeffrey knew as well as English.

As he entered the village, Jeffrey was buffeted in traffic choking the main road. Everything was in motion: bikes, scooters, cows, dogs, goats, and people. And everywhere there was sound: the metallic gnashing of gears, braying and mooing and barking, the strident hawker's voice of a scissors grinder. Jeffrey soon turned off the paved road into a dirt lane, on either side of which stood plantain, palm trees, and plaster walls fronting the courtyards of private houses. He stopped at an iron gate, unlatched it, and went inside a compound. The two-story house had once been yellow, but incessant monsoon rains had turned its sides gray with mud. There were a half-dozen mango trees in the yard, and at this time of year they were shedding leaves and the sticky petals of small yellow flowers. Looking at the littered ground, he sighed: there was plenty of work for him today. Setting his books on the porch, he could hear a voice giving brisk commands inside the house.

"Higher. Higher! Now, hold the breath. Higher! Now—hold the position!"

A broom was propped against the side of the house—an Indian broom, without a handle, consisting of bamboo strips tied together at one end. Holding this end, Jeffrey bent low and started to clean the yard. He swept with long, quick, vigorous strokes; a passerby might have thought he liked nothing better than sweeping. It was the impression Jeffrey hoped to give. The Master might have a glimpse of him from a window. If he did a slovenly, halfhearted job of sweeping, the Master would retaliate by giving him a slovenly, halfhearted lesson in Yoga. That had happened once, about a year ago, shortly after the Master had agreed to give Jeffrey lessons in exchange for work around the yard. That day, feeling lazy, Jeffrey had done a quick, indifferent job of sweeping. In turn, the Master had given him an uninspiring class for a few minutes, then sent him home.

Finished at last, Jeffrey wiped the sweat from his eyes, hearing the Master yell more commands at a student. Jeffrey smiled. At this time of day—late afternoon—the student in there would be a government official, overweight and sedentary, who had begun Yoga a few months ago on doctor's orders.

Jeffrey gathered the leaves and flower petals into a reed basket, once more appraising his work. The broom had stitched long arcs across the clay yard. He hoped

3

more leaves wouldn't fall until the Master had seen his good job. Taking the full basket behind the house, he dumped the contents into a refuse pile. At the end of the week he would burn it. Then from a well he drew up a bucket of water and took it into a shed, where, removing all his clothes, he washed thoroughly. It would not be permissible to appear rumpled and sweaty for class. In order to look neat after his chores, Jeffrey kept a supply of cotton shorts in the shed. Putting on a pair, he walked barefooted to the front porch and took up a cross-legged position on it. In the cool shade of the porch he tried to calm his mind. Under his breath, softly, he chanted a mantra, Om Namah Shivaya—Hail to Lord Shiva—again, again, and again. By fixing on each syllable of the three words, he was gradually able to exclude many thoughts of the day. For example, he had done only middling in a history test; his friend Rama broke a cricket bat during recess; the Schoolmaster, nursing a summer cold, had been snappish. Om Namah Shivaya . . . his mind steadied like a boat catching the wind in its sails. Om Namah Shivaya . . . his breath was slowing down, drawing out like a fine thread. Om Namah Shivaya . . . he was prepared for his Yoga class.

There were heavy footsteps on the floorboards of the doorway. Then out came a portly man, wearing a white shirt and a white dhoti—a long skirt of cloth. He was puffing and sweaty, his eyes bulged, his lips quivered. Jeffrey averted his eyes. It would not do to stare at the official, who was obviously exhausted. Waiting until the thickset figure had vanished into the lane, Jeffrey rose from the porch and knocked at the door, three times, faintly.

"Come in!"

4

Jeffrey opened the door, stepped inside, and without looking up fell to his knees, bending forward from the waist until his forehead touched the floor.

"Guruji," he said softly in Tamil, "I have come to beg humbly for a small portion of your time, though I have done nothing to deserve your generosity."

He made the same request every day. His father had taught him the exact words, and Jeffrey never varied them. He waited, knowing full well that the Master, as if considering the request carefully, would not reply for some moments. This too was the same every day.

Jeffrey kept his forehead pressed to the floor, his hands outspread on either side of his face, his feet and knees together. He knew the Master was studying his posture.

"Ganesh, come!" The command came with the sound of a whip cracking. In response, Jeffrey leapt instantly to his feet. The Master, a small, wiry man dressed in cotton shorts, was sipping a glass of water and fanning himself with a newspaper. It was cooler in the dim room than outside, but the heat even here was formidable.

Student and teacher went into a practice room spread with reed mats. After bowing to the Master, who sat at one end of the room, Jeffrey did some warming-up exercises. Then, on command, he performed asanas—Yoga poses—both standing and sitting. Poses that a year ago had been uncomfortable, often impossible for his body to control, were now executed with ease. Today, however, Jeffrey was apprehensive, because he was learning a difficult new asana—the Vrishchikasana. Vrishchik meant scorpion, the killer who arches its stinging tail to strike over and beyond its head. The pose therefore resembled a scorpion in the attitude of striking at its victim: body raised, balanced on forearms lying parallel on the mat; legs arched far enough backward for the feet to rest on the crown of the head. In such a position the chest, spine, and abdomen were stretched intensely until breathing became fast, labored. Jeffrey did Parivrtta Trikonasana, Paschimottanasana, Halasana, Parsvaika-pada Sarvangasana, and Salamba Sirsasana under the watchful eye of his guru, who made only slight corrections: "Hands forward," "Bring the left heel back."

Then came the order: "Now—the Vrishchikasana!"

On his first try Jeffrey lost his balance and fell on the mat. A quick glance at the Master assured him that the failure was unimportant. But then his Master never scoffed at honest failure. There would be a reprimand only if the Master sensed that his effort had been incomplete.

Jeffrey tried again, this time balancing on his forearms long enough to get his legs arched over until his feet touched the top of his head. He held the pose for a few seconds before falling out of it. Although the exertion had not seemed great, he was breathing heavily.

"Take rest," the Master said.

Instantly he lay full length on his back like a corpse, his hands palms-up a little distance from his hips, eyes closed, legs apart. He tried to loosen tension from each bundle of muscle in his body. Long practice had enabled him to relax totally within a few seconds, so that lying there he felt as though his body were elongating, lengthening into a new shape.

He was awaiting the order to perform another asana, when a new voice—young and shrill—broke the hot silence.

"Ganesh! Ganesh! Your father!"

Opening his eyes, Jeffrey saw a neighborhood boy standing in the doorway, glancing fearfully at the Master, then staring again at him.

"Ganesh!" the small boy cried. "Your father's sick! The doctor's there!"

Jeffrey would not remember how he left the room—had he even nodded respectfully to his guru?—or how he rushed into the lane. But he would remember how his legs carried him with the frustrating reluctance of a dream toward the house a kilometer away and how people turned in surprise to watch someone racing through the sweltering heat of the afternoon. Most of all he would remember the fear.

At the end of a dusty lane Jeffrey turned into the entrance of a walled little compound and collided head-on with a tall, thin man, whose breath was expelled in a grunt at the impact.

Jeffrey had nearly knocked down the village doctor.

The tall, skinny man steadied himself with one hand against the wall and moved his foot back into a sandal that had slipped off, while Jeffrey, mumbling "I'm sorry," retrieved the black medical bag that had fallen to the ground.

"Sorry . . . sorry." He gripped the satchel so tightly that the doctor had difficulty removing his hand from it. "What has happened—my father?" Jeffrey asked breathlessly.

The doctor brushed dirt from the satchel. "I haven't the equipment for tests, Ganesh, but I think your father has a little flare-up of heart trouble."

"Serious?"

The doctor cleared his throat. "We can't be sure, but

I don't think it's serious. What your father needs is to take rest. A lot of rest." The doctor grimaced. "Your father takes so little of it."

"I'll *make* him take rest," Jeffrey claimed eagerly. "What else must I do?"

The doctor shrugged and wiped some beads of sweat from his brow. "Just try to make him take rest."

"I will. I will! And thank you, doctor, thank you!" Jeffrey felt a rush of gratitude, as if he had been given a formula to cure anything. "Thank you!" he called at the tall man's back.

Out of a nearby tree a cascade of crows poured, their black wings swooping violently through the air. They startled Jeffrey; for a moment he felt a black tide of fear sweep through him, just as the crows swept through the afternoon.

He turned toward the house. It was a tiny building of plaster with a red-tiled roof. Once yellow, like the guru's house, it too was streaked gray from monsoon rains. There had been a small flower garden in the yard, but a brutal summer had wilted all the blossoms. Today the house itself looked small—dark and ugly. Jeffrey hesitated before going inside. He must not seem anxious. Taking a deep breath, he climbed two crumbling brick steps and entered the small front room that was sparsely furnished, with one picture on the wall: that of his deceased mother, a small blonde woman with delicate features and a shy smile. Jeffrey tossed his bundle of books on the table and went into his father's bedroom, where the man lay on a narrow bed, a single lumpy pillow behind his neck. Mr. Moore was slim, angular, with hawklike features and eyes even lighter blue than Jeffrey's. The overhead fan ruffled the tufts of his sandy hair. His bare chest, moving in short, rapid gusts, was freckled. The circles of his glasses glinted in light slanting through a tiny open window.

"How is the Vrishchikasana?" his father asked in English, the language they always used with each other.

"It's hard. I stayed in it a few seconds today."

"You'll master it." Father had encouraged him to study Yoga.

"I—just bumped into the doctor. I mean, I almost knocked him down."

Mr. Moore smiled wanly. "What did he say?"

"He said maybe you had a flare-up of, you know, a kind of heart trouble. That's all. He said you're okay."

"Well, I am."

"But you must take rest. You don't take enough."

Moore waved his hand feebly through the air. "Doctors always tell you the same thing. Take plenty of liquids and rest. It's the same throughout the world."

"Maybe you should go to Madras for a checkup."

"Maybe you should go take a bath. I figure what you're drenched in—and I smell—is sweat, not pure lake water."

Jeffrey knew his father would not go to Madras, yet it was worth another try. "If you have a flare-up, Dad, you must see a good doctor."

"Are there good doctors in Madras? Are there good doctors anywhere? I think our doctor here is correct. What I need is rest."

"But will you take it?"

"You go take a bath, Ganesh, while I handle my end of things by taking rest."

They smiled at each other. Jeffrey left, carrying with

him an image of his father's ashen face and weak gestures. For a moment, heading into the bathroom, he felt a surge of panic. Whom could he ask for help? Vani, their old housekeeper, would have probably influenced his father to do something more than count on a village doctor, but Vani had been dead now a year. There was the Swami himself, and Father would do what that holy man said. Except that the Swami was someone whom Jeffrey could not write. How could he ask such a holy man to come here? The Swami had renounced this world long ago, had even conducted his own death rites, for in his view he was already dead to the society of men, even though he wandered ceaselessly throughout India, visiting temples and answering the questions of people who flocked around him. The Swami would not concern himself with such an earthbound problem as sickness. A couple of years ago one of his devotees had fallen seriously ill and the Swami had never gone to him. The Swami had said, "If I am not with him now, at this moment where he is, then I cannot be with him by traveling a hundred kilometers to his bedside." Father and others had liked these words, although to Jeffrey they sounded disloyal or disinterested. At any rate, the Swami could not be counted on. Then what about the Hindu priest of the village? Father did not think much of him. And the old Irish Catholic priest who ran the Mission School would scarcely speak to Father, considering him a traitor to Christianity. So who was there to help?

In the bathroom Jeffrey removed his sweat-soaked clothes to take his second bath within an hour. Who was there to help? No one. A small house lizard, pale, almost translucent, cocked its spade-shaped head at him before vanishing like smoke into a hole near the ceiling.

*   *   *

Jeffrey Moore had lived his first nine years in the large city of Madras on the southeast coast of India. His parents had first gone there on business, but then, shaken by the plight of India's poor, had remained to work for organizations that helped the downtrodden. They traveled a lot in this service, and Jeffrey could vividly recall his mother, a frail woman, carrying a heavy knapsack into villages, somehow keeping pace with his tall, athletic father. No matter how difficult their assignment, Jeffrey accompanied them—lived in tents, mud huts, and along with them ate the poorest food of outcasts. But he remembered it all with pleasure; he remembered his parents laughing and talking and never leaving him out of their discussions. What he remembered of those first nine years of his life was so good that sometimes he wanted to go backward in time and relive them. Because not long after his ninth birthday his mother died. During a religious festival, where she went to administer anti-cholera shots to countless thousands of pilgrims, his mother contracted not cholera but encephalitis and died in a week. In the wake of that tragedy his father had brought him to this village in the south. Through the years his father had learned a lot about agriculture, applying this knowledge to the problems of district farmers. For this work an international welfare organization paid him a pittance, just enough to maintain a tiny house and hire a housekeeper-cook. After his wife's death, Mr. Moore turned to religion. He read Hindu philosophy, went to Hindu temples, practiced Hindu rituals, and after meeting the Swami became a devotee of the holy man. He followed the Swami across the face of India, often disappearing for many weeks at

11

a time. During those periods Jeffrey had been left in Vani's care; the old woman had been like a grandmother to him. After her death, Jeffrey could not count on the loyalty of new housekeepers, who came and went quickly, sometimes stealing what little there was to steal or disappearing when they could wheedle an advance on their salary out of Mr. Moore, who was generous to a fault. When his father went on a pilgrimage, Jeffrey somehow managed. Everyone in the village knew him. Out of their respect for his father's spiritual travels, the villagers looked after Jeffrey, invited him to eat at their homes, and often repaired his own little house for free. Jeffrey got along; he felt capable of always getting along, just so his father returned from the pilgrimages and told him strange tales of distant places, of the Swami and the flocks of devotees who walked from sacred temple to sacred river, living on handfuls of parched grain, drinking from streams.

Now Jeffrey was no longer confident. He was frightened by the look of his father, who in one day seemed to have lost a great deal of strength. Were his father and the doctor telling him the truth?

That night he ate with Father in his bedroom. Holding plates of rice and spiced okra on their laps, they swirled the food around with the fingertips of their right hands, Indian fashion.

Abruptly Jeffrey said, "Tell me the truth, Dad."

Sitting cross-legged on the bed, Mr. Moore began to smile in his typically cheerful way.

"Dad. Please."

"You mean about my health?"

"The truth, Dad."

Mr. Moore stared at him, then slowly lowered the plate and set it on the bed. "All right, the truth, Ganesh. The truth is I took the time on this last pilgrimage to have a checkup." Mr. Moore looked down at the plate.

Jeffrey waited, feeling sweat begin to pour down his face.

"I do have a problem," Mr. Moore continued softly. "The heart muscles are progressively weakening."

"What does that mean? Is it serious *now*?"

"Far from it." Mr. Moore's voice was cool, steady. "Eventually, over a period of time, the muscles will lose their strength."

"Over a period of time? *When?*"

"No one can say," Mr. Moore replied with a smile. "Only Tibetan monks know the exact hour they will die—and that's because they go into a death trance. They choose their time with deliberation."

"But what's a period of *time*?" Jeffrey persisted impatiently.

"Look, son, if I take care of myself, I should be around long enough to see you grown and educated. That's the truth, Ganesh, as far as I or anyone else can know."

"You should have told me about the checkup," Jeffrey said reproachfully.

"I meant to. I would have, only I've been home just a week, Ganesh." He laughed faintly. "Give me a break."

Jeffrey repeated his father's words to himself: "I should be around long enough to see you grown and educated." Jeffrey felt a little better and relaxed his hands, which he now realized had been balled tightly. "Well, you must take rest," he told his father.

"I will."

"You must not go to the fields at midday."

"I won't. You're right."

"You must take a midday nap."

"I will. I intend to do that. Now let's finish dinner."

They did, and Jeffrey took the plates out to the kitchen, where the housekeeper, a wiry little woman with gray hair, took them with a frown. She was always frowning. She never even smiled when she was paid.

When Jeffrey returned to the bedroom, he took a pillow with him—his own—to put behind his father's head.

Mr. Moore protested, then acquiesced with a smile. "Tell me, Jeffrey—" His father seldom called him by his Western name; between them it was more intimate than Ganesh, which everyone called him. Jeffrey leaned forward. "All these years I've been following Swamiji around on the pilgrimages, what did you really think?"

"It was something you had to do."

"Really? You were never angry?"

"Sometimes I was lonely," Jeffrey admitted.

"But not angry?"

"No. You had to do it."

"Do you understand why?"

"No," Jeffrey said with a grimace. "I don't like Swamiji."

"Yet you weren't angry when I followed him?"

"No. You understand him. I don't."

"Jeffrey, let me tell you something. I no longer fear death. I no longer cling to life. But I have not lost my desire to be your father. Forgive me for times when I neglected you. I wouldn't do it again. What's so clear to me now wasn't before."

"I don't care about the past," Jeffrey said. "I just want you to take rest."

For the next week Jeffrey went to school and Yoga class, while his father gradually resumed activity. Evenings they ate a simple meal of spiced vegetables and rice, then sat outside on the warm earth to watch the stars. Mr. Moore knew a lot about astronomy—indeed, he knew a lot about many things—so Jeffrey sat with him under Orion and Canis Major and listened to him expound theories about the universe, its birth, possible death, and rebirth. It was quiet in their compound, with only the hoot of owls to intrude upon their conversation or sometimes the irritable squeak of bats hanging upside down from the peepul tree. Not that the village was so peaceful outside their compound. On the main road at night there were radios playing at high decibels from almost every tea shop and milk kiosk, a constant whine of scooters, a babble of merchants around the stalls. And in village temples the priests were chanting and ringing bells to awaken the gods; from loudspeakers outside the temples poured the taped sound of devotional songs.

But in the small compound Jeffrey and his father had the broad night sky to themselves. What Jeffrey had told his father was true: he had never begrudged his father those long trips with the Swami in search of God; it was something a great man might do, and his father was a great man. Jeffrey knew this, although other people often did not. Father's acquaintances in Madras—all Westerners—had drawn away from him when he began wearing dhotis and trudging the lanes of India with a staff in hand, his sandy hair covered by a rag. Jeffrey did not understand his father either. What was a search for God, when people took to the road and followed an idea that led them nowhere, half-starved, weak, without the slightest comfort? In this village, when people sought God, they visited a Hindu temple or the Catholic chapel near the school and merely said prayers, whereas Father and other devotees exhausted themselves on the hot paths, with only a handful of rice for their daily meal. Yet Jeffrey had accepted his father's way, because that way was one of determination and courage. Jeffrey knew this and felt all right about it. And each evening that they sat together under the stars, he felt possessed by the energy of his father's presence. It seemed that nothing could break the bond between them, especially now that Father must stay close to the village. Rest would strengthen the heart muscles; Jeffrey was sure of it. Nothing ever again would stop them from sitting together under the stars in their tiny compound, walled off from the noise of the village, from the whole world.

Then one afternoon at school a neighbor appeared at the classroom door. He was a retired postal worker who had always been kind to Jeffrey. Bowing to the schoolteacher, he said, "That boy's father," and pointed to Jeffrey, who suddenly felt numb. While returning home on the back of the old man's bicycle, Jeffrey learned what had happened. There had been another "flare-up." That morning Mr. Moore had driven twenty kilometers on his scooter to inspect some irrigation ditches near a hamlet. He collapsed in a paddy, and farmers brought him home in a bullock cart.

Arriving at the compound, Jeffrey rushed into the house. The doctor had been there, but was gone now— so whispered the housekeeper to him at the front door. Father lay panting in his bedroom. Seeing his son, he waved feebly. "I was not out at midday," he said breathlessly. "It was morning. I kept my promise."

"Don't talk," Jeffrey urged. "Just take rest." Then forgetting his own words, he asked, "What did the doctor say? What happened? Does he know?"

Father smiled faintly. "Just a flare-up."

"Oh, it's more than that," Jeffrey sobbed.

"Don't worry, Ganesh, I have my pills." His father looked at the box on the little bedside table. "At the time of my checkup I got them. They're all I need."

"Don't talk, Dad, please. Take rest." Jeffrey pulled up a chair and sat quietly until his father fell asleep. Then he went outside and sat under the peepul tree. Who was around to help? He would send a letter to Swamiji anyway, that's what he'd do: "Come with help; my father's awfully sick; he has always been loyal to you, now it's your turn to be loyal to him!" Only he must not write without Father's permission; it wouldn't be fair. And would Father give it? No. Definitely not. Father would never disturb the Swami with such *unimportant* matters.

So who was there in the whole world to help? Who?

From across the yard came the retired postal worker's wife, carrying a bowl. She was a very fat woman in a brown sari.

"Tender coconut," she said, offering the bowl. "Have your father drink it. It is very good for the heart."

Jeffrey got to his feet and accepted it with thanks. The woman meant well, but every time someone in the neighborhood got sick—a cold, rheumatism, typhoid fever—she came with a bowl of tender coconut. Jeffrey took the bowl inside and placed it on the table. Then he returned to the bedroom and stared at his sleeping

17

father. One thing was sure: he would not leave the house again, not for school or Yoga or anything. If there was no one else to take care of his father, he would do it by himself.

✗   ✗   ✗

So Jeffrey stayed at home to nurse his father. At dawn he went to the village well—they had no water in their own compound—to draw water long before the housekeeper came to work, so he could make tea for Father. In the heat of midday Jeffrey gave his father a sponge bath and brought in his lunch. In the afternoon he read aloud from one of his father's philosophy books, to which his father listened intently, as if it were a rousing good story. And all through the day Jeffrey fussed with the bed sheets and pillows until his father laughed. That was something that surprised Jeffrey: how his father could still be cheerful while often in pain. Mr. Moore called Jeffrey "the little dictator" and pretended to fear his son, exclaiming, as he rolled his eyes, "Oh, my, oh, my, here he comes again!"

At night Jeffrey helped him walk slowly into the courtyard to sit against the peepul tree and look at the stars. Jeffrey never left him alone and learned to anticipate an attack—a so-called flare-up—by noticing the corners of his mouth twitch. Jeffrey would have a pill ready almost before he felt pain. Luckily the pills were effective, and within a few minutes brought relief. Each day the doctor appeared, but he was as useless as the people who came with home remedies, such as boiled nim leaves and the spiced core of plantain stalks. Still, Jeffrey was grateful for their coming. All day long they came to the broken gate of the compound with something: a few sweets, a

homemade medicine, some fruit, a plate of cooked vegetables. It was clear that the villagers were impressed by
Father, even if the Westerners in Madras had never been.
These farmers and small traders understood the fortitude
of a man who had walked the torrid roads of India seeking
God. Now, at this time of crisis, they came with their
simple marks of respect: food, remedies, a whispered in-
quiry about his health. Jeffrey forgot about the Swami.
It was enough to have these people coming to the house,
showing Father their respect.

Rama came every day after school. He was the son
of a wealthy grain merchant, and Jeffrey's best friend.
Rama was small and thin, but could wield a cricket bat
with boys twice his size. Sitting beneath the peepul tree
at sunset, the boys watched chirping bats come looping
in from somewhere, zigzagging with tremendous speed,
barreling against tree limbs to hang like bunches of dark
fruit and then whiz off again to catch insects in flight.
The boys said little, but then neither was talkative. In
better days they used to go swimming at a small lake
and dive off the backs of buffalo who stood in the water
to cool off during the afternoon heat. They hunted for
sawscale vipers—fat-tailed, little brown snakes—who in
spite of their size were aggressive killers, the cause of
more snakebite deaths than any other species in the
world. Farmers paid for the skins, each dead viper lessen-
ing their chances of stepping on a live one while plowing
the fields. The two boys would climb banyan trees to
scare monkeys, who merely scared them back, and stole
plantains from the biggest grower in the district. They
would stroll down country lanes and squint silently at
groves of bamboo and green parrots balancing on tele-
phone wires and watch the moonsoon clouds come in

like swirls of mud thrown across the bright blue sky. They were friends because they did things together, with one mind.

It was during one of Rama's visits that Mr. Moore had such a serious attack that a single pill didn't work—it took three to give him relief. Rama ran for the doctor, while Jeffrey stayed at his father's bedside, holding his cold, trembling hand, watching in agony the agony of the haggard face. When the doctor arrived, he did nothing but listen through his stethoscope. Then he shook his head gravely and declared that luckily the pills had taken effect.

Jeffrey went outside with him.

Rama was waiting there. "I am going now, Ganesh." They spoke English together.

Jeffrey nodded, although hating to see his friend leave. Still, it was right that he talk to the doctor alone.

"Sir, can my father go to Madras?"

The doctor pursed his lips without replying.

"Can it be done? Can I get him there?" Jeffrey persisted.

"I think it unlikely."

"What do you mean?"

Again the doctor paused. "I think it unlikely that your father would survive the trip. Let him rest here."

"But—isn't there *something* I can be doing?"

The doctor, who had avoided Jeffrey's eyes, now looked straight into them. "No, son, there is not. Let your father stay where he is. It's what he wants."

"How do *you* know?" Jeffrey asked bluntly, having forgotten to be polite. "How can you be knowing a thing like that!"

Quietly the doctor said, "Because he told me. Yesterday he said if it gets worse, he'd rather stay here than try

20

for Madras." The doctor touched Jeffrey's arm. "You see, a man feels better in familiar surroundings."

There were tears in Jeffrey's eyes, coming into his vision. "You mean, when he's dying? Is that what you mean?" He could not see the doctor clearly. "Is it? Is that what you mean?"

Again the doctor touched his arm. "Yes, it is. It is exactly what I mean, Ganesh."

Jeffrey wiped the tears away as the man turned and left. For a while Jeffrey stood in the courtyard, trying to get control of himself. Suddenly he thought of his mother's final illness. That had been terrible, but he had been a child then. This was worse because he was older, because no one stood between him and what was happening, as Father had stood between him and Mother's death. So he fought despair alone in the gathering twilight. Then, finally, he returned to his father's bedroom, smiling.

"Well, the doctor says—"

"I know." Father's voice was scarcely a whisper. "I know what he says."

"He says you must take more rest."

"Ganesh, sit down." He patted the bed. "It is time for more truth."

Jeffrey sat down, trying to smile.

"I love you, son. But the truth is, I am not going to be with you a lot longer."

"That's not true!"

"It is. We both know it. Don't we?"

Jeffrey felt his lips trembling so violently that he couldn't speak.

"There are things," Mr. Moore said, "we must say now."

"Don't talk, Dad. Take rest; we will talk later."

"*Now*, Jeffrey. Listen to me. In the table drawer I have put some instructions for you to follow." Mr. Moore paused for breath. "Through the years I set a little money aside for your future. Well, the future is now. Follow my instructions. They'll take you—" Again he paused. "To a man in Madras who'll make arrangements."

"For what, Dad?"

"For going to America." Mr. Moore placed his trembling hand on Jeffrey's arm. "Your aunt has always wanted you to live with her."

Jeffrey knew this. His aunt, a widow, often wrote and pleaded for him to come to America.

"I want you to go," said Father.

"I don't want to leave you or India."

"Dear Jeffrey, I am going to leave you whether we like it or not."

Jeffrey could hold back no longer; he put his head in his hands and sobbed.

"Look, son, I told you I'm not afraid of dying. You alone worry me. I want you to leave here for a while. For education, experience. Come back later—" He paused for breath. "But after trying another life. You owe it to yourself. I promised your mother—"

"I don't want to leave."

"Promise you will follow my instructions!" Mr. Moore raised up on his elbows, panting, his face ashen and contorted.

Jeffrey, frightened, begged him to lie back. "I promise," he said hastily. "Now take rest. Please! I promise!"

Mr. Moore sighed and fell back against the pillows. Then he winked at Jeffrey. "I trapped you, didn't I. I

22

took unfair advantage. Just the same, you promised. Jeffrey, you promised!"

✗   ✗   ✗

A week passed without anything eventful happening, without a single attack, so that Jeffrey regained his hope. Father was in good spirits too, as if suffering from nothing more than a summer cold. He rested quietly through the day, and at night, holding Jeffrey's arm, he shuffled outside to sit under the peepul tree. Once he said, "I can't blame you for disliking Swamiji. He took up time I should have given to you. Now I no longer need him. But it took years for me to learn my answer is not in him but in myself. And in you, Jeffrey, and in the bats flying around, and the farmers of this village, and in whoever is laughing out there. We are all the same consciousness."

At another time he said, "Remember this, Jeffrey. The soul is a bird. The nest it makes is the body. A bird makes its nest, raises its fledglings, then flies away. The nest rots, but the bird has made another nest. That is life and rebirth, son. Forgive my lecturing you, but there isn't time to come to things naturally."

And he said, "Work hard, Jeffrey. Not for any reason but the work being given to you. Do the work with detachment—do it because it is your work, and for no other reason. Remember I said this."

And one night, smiling, he said, "Isn't tomorrow Divali?"

It was Divali, India's major festival, celebrating the triumph of good over evil. "I guess it is," Jeffrey said.

"You *guess* it is? Where are you going to celebrate it?"

"Nowhere."

"Hasn't anyone asked you to his house?"

"Well, Rama—"

"Then go."

"No, I will not, Dad."

"Don't you want to go?"

Jeffrey shook his head, although the truth was he hated to miss Divali. It was a celebration that he and his schoolmates looked forward to for months.

"Jeffrey, go."

"I would rather stay here."

"Go to Rama's house. Go on. Divali is a wonderful time. Enjoy it. Go to Rama."

And so at sunset the next day, having fluffed his father's pillow and straightened the bed sheet, Jeffrey prepared to leave for the celebration. He promised to stay only an hour and again insisted that he didn't really want to go, although his heart was beating fast at the sound of fireworks popping off in the distance.

For a moment he held his father's hand, then rushed into the gathering dusk. He passed through the center of the village, where festivities, started days ago, were reaching their climax this night. There was a low cloud of acrid smoke in the furious streets. Every shop was strung with colored lights—his father had once said it looked like Christmas in America. A young man was setting off a string of firecrackers that jerked and danced around the feet of squealing girls. Farmers were arriving from outlying districts to see the display and drink strong toddy; their bike bells made a constant tinkling sound along the main road. Vendors, smoking cigars, were selling peacock feathers, sweetmeats, and bright silk saris. Jeffrey waved at some boys from school who were crowded near a tea shop, smirking and looking suspicious

as doubtless they were getting ready to set off a fusil-
lade of spinners and twisters.

Leaving the main thoroughfare, Jeffrey headed down
a small lane; the sudden quiet sobered him. Should he
have left tonight? He had vowed never to leave, but
then Father had insisted that he go. There hadn't been
a single flare-up for days; this afternoon there had been
a little color in Father's cheeks. Yet why had he left the
house? Because it was terribly grim being cooped up
so long—and because this was Divali!

He went on down the lane, whistling a jaunty tune
to fit the evening. Firecrackers went off behind a compound wall. Ahead he saw a swish of blue flame, a riot
of reds and greens, as a rocket exploded above the palm
trees. Then he turned into Rama's compound. The house
was large—three stories—with a garage too, for Rama's
father was one of only eight men in the village who
owned automobiles. Rama and his four brothers were
already in the yard, holding sparklers with which they
lit off rockets, dazzlers, and spinners, creating a wall of
sound and light beyond the vast flowerbeds. Rama rushed
to meet him and thrust a lit sparkler into his hand. Soon
they were both setting off a variety of fireworks, while
servants brought out trays of sweet rice and raisin curd.
Rama's father, dressed in slacks and a polo shirt, officiated
when the dangerous cherry bombs went off with ear-
splitting explosions. Thereafter the whole neighborhood
lit up with shooting rays of fire and wriggling trails of
glitter. Rama's great-grandmother sat on the long porch,
mouthing her toothless gums, enjoying the color, the
motion. Inside the house Rama's mother and grandmother were in the kitchen, supervising the preparation
of more food. Later there would be gifts and games, and

25

visitors from throughout the village would come for a songfest.

Holding a sparkler, Jeffrey glanced at Rama, who smiled back, and then at Rama's father, who bent down to light a spinner. Rama's father . . . Rama's father . . . *Father*.

Jeffrey felt a rush of cold air blow across his forehead. He dropped the sparkler, turned, and ran.

"Where are you going?" Rama called at his back. "Ganesh!"

But Jeffrey was rushing through the night shattered by detonations that sent thunder into the sky and great bursts of brilliant light.

When he reached the broken gate of the compound, he breathed a sigh of relief, for all the way home he had imagined that the house had been set on fire by a wayward firecracker. There was only an electric light shining inside the tiny house—Father was safe. For a moment Jeffrey almost turned and went back to Rama's. At least he should look in on Father, having come all this way, so he entered the house and saw, from the doorway, a man standing in his father's bedroom.

It was a temple priest with whom Father often talked about God.

Dressed only in a dhoti, the man stood by the bed with his hands held together in the attitude of prayer. He was speaking. Was he talking to Father? Or chanting?

Slowly Jeffrey drew nearer and saw, to the right of the priest, the head of Father, eyes closed.

Jeffrey leapt forward.

The priest, startled, turned and stepped aside, so that Jeffrey had a full view of his father. Eyes closed, lips compressed.

26

"Some time ago," the priest explained quietly, "the housekeeper found him, Ganesh. Then sent for me."

"Some time ago?" Jeffrey wondered how long he had been gone. He came to the bed and looked down. It was his father, only the face seemed pinched and smaller, the long, hawklike nose sharper, without any flesh at all. Jeffrey's lips trembled.

"This was in his hand." The priest gave a lined sheet of yellow paper to Jeffrey. "He must have been writing when it happened."

Jeffrey read: "A holy man once said, 'I am supposed to be dying. But how can I die? I am here!' "

Jeffrey looked at the priest.

"It is very auspicious," the priest said.

Jeffrey clutched the sheet of paper and reread it; the scrawled words swam in front of his eyes. Glancing up, he was astonished to see the parchmentlike gray skin of his father's face. It was and was not his father. It wasn't fair for him to look like that—so gray, so distant, so unreal. The priest was talking quietly, as if of the weather: Mr. Moore, being who he was, would be given the rites of a Brahman, with certain omissions, of course, since he had never been invested with the sacred thread of that caste. Just the same, Mr. Moore had lived a good life and had done good work and, most important, had traveled on many pilgrimages with the Swami, and at the time of his death had written down auspicious words, so tomorrow a modified Brahman funeral would be given him.

Jeffrey slumped to the floor, rocking slowly. His father was gray, eyes closed, lips compressed. His father was dead.

"I have sent for assistance from the temple," said the

priest. "They will help with everything. I have also in-formed the cremator. Ganesh?"

Jeffrey looked up at the heavyset priest, whose head was shaved, aside from a topknot of long black hair. There were three ash marks across his forehead; he was a devotee of Shiva. What had the man said?

"Ganesh," said the priest. "The funeral. We will need money for it."

Listlessly the boy nodded.

"Do you have the money now?"

Jeffrey waved his hand vaguely and continued rocking.

"Will you have it then tomorrow?"

Jeffrey nodded.

"In the morning?"

He nodded.

"Because people must be paid. There is firewood and ghee for the fire and flowers to be bought. First thing in the morning?"

Jeffrey nodded.

The room became still, not even a fly buzzing to break the silence, and Jeffrey thought the priest had left.

Then behind him came the low, gentle voice. "Ganesh, go to your own room tonight. Do not stay here."

Jeffrey nodded, but without moving. He would stay in his father's room tonight. "What time is it, sir?" he asked the priest, without looking up.

The priest told him.

So, Jeffrey thought grimly, he had left the house more than two hours ago. If he had returned on time, as prom-ised, he might have seen his father alive. Could he ever forgive himself? Just for some fireworks, for sweets, ex-citement.

Looking at the paper, which, in his grip, was now crumpled, he read the words again. The last word, "here," was badly scrawled and the exclamation mark scooted off the page. Had Father written it when the attack came? What did the priest mean by "auspicious"? The word meant "favorable," and in Hindu usage a promising outcome for the soul. Yes, but *what* soul! There was no soul. Swami and the others had not helped Father when he needed it. They did nothing, those men in search of God. All they had done was exhaust Father on all those pilgrimages, leading him from temple to temple until his heart gave out.

"I am supposed to be dying. But how can I die? I am here!"

But Father was not here. Something lay on the bed, growing pinched and small, its color changing into the metallic hue of a rock.

Jeffrey stretched out on the floor, staring at overhead cracks in the glare of a naked light bulb. "But how can I die?" Father had died; he was not here. But the priest had said "auspicious." Maybe Father had not really died; maybe he was still here. But Jeffrey felt no presence save his own, his own that had betrayed the most important of trusts. He had given up the last precious moments with his father for a couple of firecrackers.

✶   ✶   ✶

Before dawn he awoke, with the light still on and people moving about the room. The scent of flowers and sandalwood paste filled the air, along with the murmur of chanting voices; outside the open window the strident call of crows had begun, bringing, as usual, the first sound of morning into a village compound. Jeffrey got up and rubbed his eyes. He dared to look at his father, whose

29

face was nearly hidden beneath lotus petals. Two old women had apparently dressed the body in a clean white dhoti and placed about the neck a garland of fresh flowers. The priest sat crosslegged in a corner, bent over a Sanskrit prayer book, mumbling rapidly.

Jeffrey left the room, bathed, and changed into a dhoti himself. He knew how to handle the long piece of cloth, how to air the "wings" of a dhoti, which, untucked, reached to the ankles. Like any Indian, he knew how to fight the midday heat by pulling the cloth folds loose from the waist and spreading them to the breeze. Now, however, just at dawn, the air was almost cool. Jeffrey brushed his teeth with a stick in the yard and as usual went to the small chicken coop to see if the hen had laid any eggs. He did not let himself think; he simply moved through the early light, watching one foot go before the other. It was almost cool, his father was dead, there was a single egg in the hen house, his father was dead, the crows were now setting up a terrible racket in the peepul tree, his father was dead.

He couldn't stop himself from thinking, "I am here." Where? Had Father meant hovering around the bedroom or wandering through the village or beyond into the land of India or into space, or had he meant being here in an abstract way, like a principle, a spirit or soul described in a book? Ideas caught in the flow of Jeffrey's mind like a logjam. He tried to break them free, but they remained stuck, letting other impressions flow past, unable to break free themselves and go on. "I am here." In the bedroom? On earth? In the cosmos? With God? Who was God or what was God—and did it really matter to Father, now that he lay wreathed in flowers with sandalwood paste rubbed into his gray skin, his hands unable to brush the flies away?

All morning Jeffrey sat in the front room, while people came to pay their respects. When Rama came, he looked shy and guilty—doubtless recalling their mutual gaiety at the precise moment when a man died. The two boys went outside together and stood under the peepul tree in the gathering heat. They were silent awhile. Finally Rama said, "Ganesh, where will you go?"

Jeffrey shrugged. "I can't think of it now."

"I hope you stay here."

"That's what I want to do."

Both boys looked at the ground, scuffing their sandals in the dust.

"Father wanted me to leave," Jeffrey said.

"Yes, I suppose he would."

Jeffrey looked at his friend in surprise. "Why would he?"

"If he wasn't here with you, he'd want you to go home."

"But this *is* home." Jeffrey tapped the earth with his foot. "Right here."

"That's true. And yet—"

"Don't I belong here? Rama?"

"Of course. As much as I do. I hope you always stay here, because you are my friend. Only—"

"Only what?" Jeffrey persisted.

"It will be different without your father."

"I always got along when he was away."

"But everyone knew he was coming back."

Jeffrey thought about that. "Rama, what are you really telling me?"

"Well, some people will think you don't belong in the village anymore." Rama stared at the ground.

"I have lived here five years."

"Yes, but these people have lived here for generations. And—you're a foreigner."

"I'm an Indian!"

Rama shook his head sadly. "Some people won't see you that way. I can. I will. But they won't. They'll say you should go, now that your father no longer goes with Swamiji on pilgrimages. Thing is, people will treat you differently."

"I don't believe it."

Staring at the ground hard for a few moments, Rama then reached out and gripped his friend's arm. "You are closer to me than my own brothers. I will never forget you." With that he walked away, head down, feet dragging, his hands thrust deep into his pockets.

Then the priest called Jeffrey aside. "It is very hot today, Ganesh. I have talked to Subish. You know Subish?"

Jeffrey nodded. Subish was a tea-shop owner who doubled as the village cremator.

"Subish says we should do it this evening."

"So soon?" The idea of having the funeral this very day was overwhelming to Jeffrey. "Why not wait at least until tomorrow?"

"Tomorrow will be uncomfortable." Jeffrey understood "uncomfortable." The priest meant that in this heat the body would begin to smell. The idea sickened him: his father stinking.

Earlier this morning, after eating a rice cake for breakfast, Jeffrey had taken the instructions from the table drawer. They had led him to a strongbox buried near the hen house; he had opened it with a key taped to the instructions. He had never known Father to be so thorough and detailed about practical matters. From a large cache of rupee notes inside the box, Jeffrey had taken enough to pay the priest and others. Then he had closed the box again and—following instructions—had locked it with a small chain to an iron ring, which had been used long ago to tie a bull next to the hen house. Then he had piled some leaves over the box and left it.

Now that the priest and his assistants had their pay, they were in a hurry to finish the task.

"Then this evening," Jeffrey agreed listlessly.

With a sigh the priest hurried to make sure that preparations, already under way, proceeded quickly. Returning to the front room in sweltering heat (there was no fan), Jeffrey received more people from the village. They entered silently, holding their hands in prayer, often prostrating themselves before the bed of his father.

Rama is wrong, he thought. These people will not let me down.

✗   ✗   ✗

In late afternoon with shadows inching up the gray sides of the tiny house, the stretcher arrived, carried by four strong young men. It had been decorated with flowers. Jeffrey clenched his fists, as they lifted his father's body and placed it on the stretcher. A flutist and a drummer had been hired by the priest to furnish music for the funeral procession. They grinned at Jeffrey and their red-rimmed eyes suggested that they had already been drinking. Other men, gathering for the procession, were drinking from a bottle. It was arrack, a strong liquor made of fermented palm juice. The arrack was colorless like

33

water, but when they drank it, they gasped and wheezed.

"Ganesh," said the priest and thrust a lit oil lamp into his hands. "I brought the flame from the temple."

"Thank you," Jeffrey said gratefully. He himself must light the funeral pyre; it would not do to use any flame but a sacred one. The priest had been thoughtful to bring this fire from the temple.

The procession of a score of men, with the pallet in their midst, set out to the lively beat of the drummer. The priest led the way, with Jeffrey just behind him, carrying the lamp, which actually was a deep brass dish of oil with a wick floating in it. As they moved into the lane, people came to their compound gates and silently watched. A few small boys joined in, racing alongside the pallet, studying the drummer, whose two-headed drum hung from a strap around his neck. Some of the men, passing the bottle, began a shuffling little dance in the dusty road. They snapped their fingers and preened like fighting cocks with wings flared; they circled one another, their faces rapt in solemn concentration upon the movement. Then the flute began accompanying the drum; it was a long flute of bamboo, and the player ran the scales effortlessly in a carefree rhythm, its sound thin and reedy. More people lined the road, some of them joining the procession, passing bottles of arrack. Some threw flowers in the path of the mourners.

Jeffrey looked straight ahead, walking carefully in order to keep the oil from spilling. This was his job, to carry the flame. He must concentrate on doing it. He must think of nothing else. Yet the outer world impinged upon him: he saw curious or solemn faces in front of doorways and heard behind him the rhythm of flute and drum, and he knew, even without looking, that some of the men were dancing, for like the small boys accompanying him, he too had followed such processions.

The procession snaked through the main market, drawing glances from merchants, from men drinking tea in dark stalls. Scooters revved up indifferently, radios screeched. More men joined the dancers until a full dozen were leaping and kicking in front of the borne stretcher. Jeffrey tried to think only of the flame jetting from the deep brass dish, but in painful flashes he imagined what was behind, not ten steps away: his garlanded father on a pallet, being drawn through the casual village streets toward incineration.

Then the procession broke free of the daily business of the village and emerged on a high road leading toward the nearby river where the local crematory was. Through the fading sunlight Jeffrey had a sudden glimpse between trees of the laid pyre, and for a moment he thought his legs might give way. Look at the flame. Remember the flame. Guard the flame.

Once the cavalcade reached the outer boundary of the crematorium grounds, drum and flute ceased playing, the dancers drifted away, the mood became solemn. Every eye was fixed on the pyre, which had been constructed of alternate layers of cow-dung cakes—to preserve the fire's heat—and oak logs, until it stood chest high.

Jeffrey saw the cremator standing next to the cement platform on which the pyre had been built. Sporting a goatee, Subish gave him a smile. He was a spindly-legged man in a dirty pair of khaki shorts, no shirt at all, and a frayed sailor's cap set jauntily back on his head. His odd, rumpled, carefree look annoyed Jeffrey. Subish could have taken better care of his appearance.

The bearers gently lifted the corpse from the pallet

and placed it on the top layer of logs.

"I am here," flashed through Jeffrey's mind. He fought back tears. To steady himself, he stared hard at the flame dancing on the surface of the colorless oil.

For a while Subish and other men worked at completing the pyre by building up a few more alternating layers of cow-dung cakes and oak logs to surround and cover the corpse. They left uncovered a space directly over the dead man's chest and face. All that Jeffrey heard, during this time, was the thud of log on log, the men's breathing, the wind shaking the leaves of an ashoka tree that stood near the riverbank. Often he glanced down at the flame blown sideways by gusts of wind. He concentrated on the yellow conical shape to keep his mind steady. There was always the mantra—Om Namah Shivaya—that he used to steady his mind for Yoga, but now he could invoke none of the gods. The gods had betrayed him.

At last the pyre was completed. The priest walked forward and chanted verses from the Hindu scriptures, while Subish carried a bucket of melted ghee—concentrated butter—around the pyre, splashing the logs with it so they would ignite quickly. Bending down, the priest took a handful of flowers from a large basket and threw them on the pyre. Other people followed, tossing blossoms, bowing their heads. At last Jeffrey bent over the basket; his hand, reaching for some petals, trembled violently. With white and purple petals clutched in his fingers, he walked to the pyre and let the sweet-smelling flowers sift over his dead father's face. He wanted to say something. Long afterward he would recall this moment and realize that he had wanted to question his father. Where are you? Are you really here? Your face says no. There is nothing in it. Why did you say, "How can I die? I am here"?

Jeffrey stepped back to make way for the priest, who did more chanting. Meanwhile, from a nearby shed, Subish brought an earthenware jar, holding it with two thick pads of cloth, and placed it at Jeffrey's feet. Inside the jar were glowing coals.

Jeffrey knew what to do. He took the cloth pads from Subish and gripped the sides. Lifting the jar carefully, he walked to the pyre and held it over the dead man's exposed chest. Slowly tilting the jar, he poured the live coals out.

Stepping back, he looked around for a stone. Subish pointed to one set in the ground for this purpose. Jeffrey threw the jar hard against the stone, breaking it into ochre shards.

When the priest nodded, Jeffrey picked up the oil lamp, noticing his hands no longer trembled. The ritual had steadied them. "I am doing it, Dad," he said to himself. "I am doing it right."

Subish brought forward a long stick wrapped at one end with cloth soaked in ghee. Jeffrey touched the end of it to the lamp wick. With a tiny whoosh, flame spread along the cloth until the stick became a firebrand. Again the priest nodded, so Jeffrey stepped up and without hesitation held the torch to one side of the pyre. With a greater whoosh the flame billowed up from the ghee-soaked logs. He moved to the opposite side and applied the torch there. Within seconds the whole pyre was engulfed in furious yellow light, and the intense heat made onlookers step back. Jeffrey glanced at them. Not one person was looking at the pyre. They feared that their attention would hold the dead man's soul in bondage to the earth. But Jeffrey looked. Through skeins of flame and complex layers of logs and cow dung, he saw the interior bundle. People could not hold down Father's spirit—if Father had one. If Father had a spirit, it would rise on its own power and nothing could stop it. If Father had one. Did Father have a soul, a spirit, something lasting? Was he here?

"I am here."

It was not so. Jeffrey sat down on the earth, while flames rose briskly into the twilight, and the heat from the conflagration added to that of the sultry afternoon, causing sweat to pour in rivulets down his face.

The priest squatted beside him. "Ganesh, don't look."

"I must."

Without glancing at the pyre, the priest grimaced and rose with a sigh. Along with the others he left the crematorium grounds. No one but Subish, the keeper of this place, would stay while the blaze was in its fury. Only at dawn would the others return, when there was nothing here but ashes.

Jeffrey looked. He sat in the full lotus position of Padmasana, learned painfully and patiently with his guru, and stared at the burning pyre, its dark parcel inside the maze of logs and cow-dung cakes. The sun had set, but he hadn't noticed, so intent was his mind on the processes of cremation. He would not glance away. This was happening to his father; he must therefore experience it. He did not avert his eyes even when, to his horror, enormous blisters formed on the corpse. Flowers and dhoti had burned off, leaving the body itself fully exposed, the limbs and trunk seething in flames. The terrible blisters expanded and popped with a put-put sound that

Jeffrey would never forget. He watched the interior liquids begin to ooze from the broken blisters, then gush forth like springs from the earth.

"I am here."

Minutes later, when the sizzling liquids stopped flowing, it seemed to Jeffrey that the corpse had shrunk greatly in size—nothing but bones now, and tatters of flesh that had turned a ghastly white, the color of chalk. Tears filled Jeffrey's eyes, but he continued to look. He must not draw back from what was happening to his father. Or to the corpse. To his father, to the corpse. To both? Or only one?

Time passed while the wood split and crackled on the pyre, the snaky rising of flame almost hypnotizing Jeffrey. He had no sense of time anymore, no awareness of how long he was there before the corpse sat up.

His father sat up. Right up, as if rising from bed. Trunk and head lifted from the pyre, scattering logs in the rising.

Jeffrey leapt to his feet, yelling, "Dad! Dad!"

Out of nowhere came Subish, wielding a large club. With swift, powerful blows he beat the corpse down. Jeffrey rushed at him. "Don't hit my father! Don't you hit my father!"

Subish paid no attention, but kept battering the corpse until it lay flat on the logs, each blow loosening from the dark body a glitter of sparks. Then he turned and motioned Jeffrey away. "Sit over there if you're staying! Otherwise go home! I'm in charge here!"

Sobered by this command, Jeffrey backed away and sat down. He was trembling and sobbing, unable to believe what had happened. "I am here." Is that what Father meant, that he would rise from the burning? That it would take a club to put him down again? Of course not. "I am here." The words meant nothing. They were a lie.

Finally Subish came over and sat down beside him. "Forgive my shouting at you, Ganesh. You just saw something few people ever see. It's a good thing too. It would upset the families. Better they don't see."

"My father—sat up."

Subish chuckled and used his frayed sailor cap to wipe his sweaty brow. He had a bald head that glistened like mahogany in the firelight. "Not your father, Ganesh. It wasn't he who sat up. That was only the body tightening up when it lost its moisture. Happens every time. In the big cities, they tie the bodies to the logs with baling wire, but here we do it the old way. Why, I've seen them jump up and look like they were going to run away!" He added quickly, "Forgive me. Sometimes I speak thoughtlessly."

Jeffrey reached out and touched the man's sweaty arm. "Forgive me, Subish, for shouting. For a moment there, I—"

"You hoped."

Jeffrey nodded, brushing the sweat from his face. "I think I did. For a moment."

"Well, you must not look for your father here."

Jeffrey stared at the cremator, who until this moment had never impressed him one way or another, except to annoy him today by wearing a sailor's hat and a pair of dirty shorts. Now Jeffrey studied the bony face, the wispy goatee, the smile made singular by two missing front teeth, the kind and steady eyes. The eyes held him— they meant more than all the rest of Subish.

"Where must I look for him then?" asked Jeffrey.

Subish shrugged. "Go to the temple like others. Ask

Lord Shiva. Ask Lord Krishna. Ask the goddess Devi. Ask the god whose name you are known by—ask Ganesh. The gods know. I certainly do not."

"But what do you think happens?" Jeffrey persisted. "You have gone through this many times. You see the bodies sit up. What do you think?"

"Me? I do my work. I am paid for it. Tomorrow, after I clean up the platform, I will bathe in the river, buy some arrack, drink, and have a good snooze. It's always the same with me. I let the gods take care of the rest."

✗　　✗　　✗

The last that Jeffrey remembered of the long night was the look of the flames, how imperceptibly they grew smaller, their dancing less violent, until he could no longer see an object embedded in them, only a vast liquid basin of shimmering orange. He felt a kind of peace settle around him, as if the dying flames brought calm. The only sound at the crematory was that of crickets singing and, infrequently, the distant hoot of an owl. Subish had long since fallen asleep, making of his sailor's hat a tiny pillow. His goatee was a smear of darkness against his otherwise glowing skin in the firelight. Jeffrey nodded—flames, then darkness.

Abruptly Jeffrey awoke to the sound of crows. A squabbling group of them had nested in a nearby tree; when he opened his eyes, the first thing he saw was a huge, ugly-beaked crow balancing on a limb too small for its great bulk.

Jeffrey sat up. There were no more flames, no fire at all, but smoke rising from the collapsed mass of logs. It was hard to believe that yesterday the crossed logs had risen to the height of a man's chest. Now they resolved themselves into a mound no more than a few inches deep.

Subish was already up and around. He came from the river, his body dripping. "Good morning, Ganesh," he said cheerfully, as if they had never shared such a terrible watch together. "Go down and see the fog."

Jeffrey got up. His legs were stiff in the moist, cool morning. He walked to the riverbank and watched puffs of fog roll away from a grove of bamboo. The gray ephemeral tentacles slowly let go of the thin trunks and faded into the soft flow of orange light that would soon turn a brilliant red in the east. Jeffrey walked into the water, into its cooling freshness. Behind him the crows cawed raucously and across the river a cow mooed as it greeted the day. Jeffrey looked up. A sliver of moon still shone faintly in the sky, tilting the vast canopy between night and day. He felt good. He felt wonderful. There had never been such a beautiful morning.

When he returned to the pyre, the priest had arrived along with a dozen other people—farmers who had known Jeffrey's father.

"Are you ready, Ganesh?" the priest asked gently.

"I am ready."

"Did you stay here all night?" When Jeffrey nodded, the priest shrugged. "Put it on my head, please." He meant an earthenware jug at his feet. Ganesh lifted it and gave it to the priest, who held it with both hands on his head. Subish followed the priest to the smoking pyre and at his command knocked a little hole in the side of the jug with a sharply pointed rock. Water poured out. Still holding the jug on his head, the priest tilted it toward the heap of ashes. He moved from one side to another, until the ashes of the corpse were thoroughly wet.

Jeffrey thought, Some of the ashes are from the logs, not Father. Does it matter? How can it matter? How can it not matter?

Setting the jug down, the priest bent over a central mound of ashes—hardly more than a handful—and worked diligently for a while. Finished, he stepped back and called Jeffrey, who saw the crude doll-like shape of a man that the priest had fashioned from the moist ashes.

"Get me the milk, Subish," said the priest, looking pleased with his artistry. Subish handed him another jug, which he held over the ashes shaped like a man's body. Reciting some verses, he then poured out the milk, which, in the feathery ashes, made little holes, like rain pattering into dust. With the sacred milk he had purified the ashes and removed from them all the sins of the man.

"It is done," sighed the priest, turning to Jeffrey. "Now collect the ashes and take them to the river."

"Not this river."

"Why not?"

"I must take them to the Cauvery."

"Yes, that is a very sacred river," the priest said thoughtfully. "But you will have to pay money to get there. Can you pay for the bus ride?"

"Let the boy do what he wants," put in Subish. "Anyway, foreigners always have money."

Jeffrey started. It was the first time in his memory that a villager had ever called him a foreigner.

"Then, if you have bus fare," said the priest, "go to the Cauvery. It is more sacred there than here."

At the word "here," Jeffrey glanced quickly at the wet little mound of ashes. Then he said, "Do you have a metal jar, Subish? For the journey?"

"I do. A copper one. With a thick cloth cover that we can seal with wax. But it will cost you five rupees."

Jeffrey turned to the pyre and stared again at the ashes. In a few minutes he would be scooping them into a copper pot. Maybe two handfuls altogether. His father.

"I am here."

At this moment Jeffrey felt a terrible despair; it was like a hand seizing hold of his body and draining him of strength. Only two handfuls of ashes. The man he had loved, admired, worried over—the man he had wanted to keep here with him always. Always here! Next to him, standing *right here!* Two handfuls of ashes.

✳ **✳** **✳**

For the next few days Jeffrey stayed home, sleeping most of the time as if exhausted after tremendous physical labor. He slept in his own tiny room and kept the door closed to his father's bedroom. He had forgotten about school and Yoga classes; they existed in another world at another time, when he had belonged to this village. Rama had been right: he belonged to it no longer. His friend had spoken the truth, more anxious to be honest than obliging. On the day after the funeral, people started coming to the house and asking if he had anything foreign to sell. They were blunt; the respectful deference of the mourning had gone up in the smoke of the pyre. Even the retired postal worker and his wife came to ask if there were anything foreign he wished to sell. Jeffrey had nothing to sell—there was nothing of value in this household, foreign or otherwise—but the idea of his neighbors asking him, as if they were confident of his going away for good, intensified the sense of loneliness and isolation that had been his ever since he scooped the ashes into a copper pot.

On the third day the housekeeper told him she would be leaving. After tomorrow she would no longer work or cook for him. Why? Because it was bad luck to work in such a house. She had only stayed this long because of respect for his father and a liking for him. But she could not stay longer; her neighbors would think less of her for working in such a house, with only a boy for master. Then on that same day the landlord appeared, a short man with thin arms and an immense paunch. Though clean, his dhoti was rumpled across the flab of his great belly. He wanted a month's rent in advance. When Jeffrey observed that the rent was paid until the end of next week, the landlord snapped, "I know it, but I cannot keep the house for you after that date, unless I have both the next month's rent and another month's in advance."

"But, sir, why?"

"You are here all alone?"

"Yes, sir."

The fat man snorted. "Who knows what a lone boy will do in a house? Boys are irresponsible enough when they are not alone. You might play with matches, burn it down, do anything. I must protect my interests. I mean nothing against you personally, Ganesh; you have always been a nice boy. But this is business."

Later that day the old Irish priest who ran the Mission School came to the house. He wanted to know when Jeffrey was leaving.

"I haven't thought about it, Father."

45

"Well then, lad, you'd better. It's more than three weeks of school you've been missing, and with good reason, to be sure, but you can't go on this way. You need someone to look after you, Jeffrey. You need to go back to your own country and take hold."

Jeffrey understood that by "taking hold" the old priest meant taking hold of the Christian faith again and renouncing the alien gods of his father.

It was after this conversation that Jeffrey left his house for the first time since the funeral. He went to see Rama.

They sat on the back porch of the large, rambling house, while two of Rama's brothers played badminton on the lawn.

"I'm sorry," Jeffrey began, when his friend handed him a bottle of Orange Fanta. "You said people would change, but I didn't believe you. I just got angry. Now I know it's true."

Rama nodded. "We are village people. My father says life is narrow here. He complains of it, but his work is in this district, so we'll never leave."

"I see now that everything depended on my father. What people thought of him. Otherwise we could never have stayed and people would never have treated me as one of them."

"People thought your father was a god-man. And you were liked too."

"Now they want me gone."

"It's that they don't know what to do, Ganesh. You're alone, and it puzzles them. Everyone has someone in India. If a man dies, his son can always count on uncles, brothers, cousins. But you can't, Ganesh, and people don't know who you are anymore—except a foreigner." He added shyly, "That's what my father says."

Jeffrey sipped the Fanta, avoiding his friend's eyes. He couldn't understand why, but he felt somehow ashamed. Here he had always been Rama's equal, but now he was beneath his friend. He was unwanted.

"My father says you can come live with us."

Jeffrey looked up and saw Rama smiling.

"That's what my father said. At breakfast this morning he said it. He said, 'Rama, tell him to come here.' I was going to tell you today."

Jeffrey stared at his small, thin friend, whose eyes were brilliant in anticipation of his acceptance. And Jeffrey almost leapt up and shouted "Yes! I will come here! This very day!" Almost, but something held him back. For a moment he didn't even know what it was. He had tried to forget it, the promise made to his father during those last days together. Until this moment, when he had the chance to stay here, Jeffrey hadn't thought about it, had put it out of his mind whenever the idea of going to America nudged forward. He wanted to accept the offer, because he knew Rama's father was a man who meant what he said. Jeffrey got along with his friend's mother and four brothers too. He could envision a good life with them: walking to school with Rama, coming back again, eating with the family, playing cricket with the boys, enjoying the peace of this large safe compound.

Jeffrey got to his feet. "I will never forget your offer," he said. "I thank you, Rama. I thank your father. But—I am going to leave, just as people expect me to do."

Rama rose, frowning. "Forget what people say! My father is known here. If you live with us, it will be the same as it was. They won't dare to call you a foreigner!"

"No, I have a promise to keep."

"What promise?"

"Made to my father before he died. That I would go to America."

"You promised him?"

"So I must keep my word."

Rama nodded. "Yes, I would feel the same."

The boys looked sorrowfully at each other.

"When must you leave?"

"I am going tomorrow. First to Trichy and the Cauvery River. With the ashes."

"Yes, I see."

"Then by train to Madras to look up a man who'll help me reach America."

"Do you need money?"

"No, my father left me enough." Jeffrey laughed faintly. "I think it was the first time in his life he ever saved money for anything."

"Are you sure you have enough?"

"I'm sure. Thank you—" Jeffrey didn't know what else to say.

Rama bit his lip and said, "Write me."

"I always will. All my life."

"That is a promise?"

"Of course!"

"Because you keep promises, Ganesh."

"I promise. And you?"

"I promise!"

×　　　×　　　×

That evening Jeffrey packed his one suitcase, having scarcely enough things to fill it. He kept his Sanskrit dictionary, but decided to leave his school books—he would not have time to look at them before arriving in America, and then he would probably have new ones.

America. He would not think about it now. That would come later. He then rolled a small bronze statue in a pair of pants and placed it in the suitcase. On his last birthday Jeffrey had been given this statue by his father. It was a replica of the god whose name he went by in the village: Ganesh, son of Shiva, with the head of an elephant, the body of a fat man, and four arms holding a club, a noose, a rice cake, and a broken tusk. On the base of the statue crouched a rat, the god's servant, looking reverently up at him. Ganesh was a strange-looking figure—half man, half elephant—but for someone raised in such knowledge, the god represented both strength and wisdom. An elephant's trunk could uproot a tree or discriminate among peanuts, sifting through them to find the best one. The enormous belly represented the universe or knowledge, depending upon the interpretation. His servant, the rat, could gnaw through most obstacles, just as an elephant could push aside whatever lay in its path. That is why Ganesh was sometimes called Vinayaka, Remover of Obstacles; and sometimes Akhuratha, He Who Rides a Rat; or Heramba, Protector, along with a dozen other names, all of which Jeffrey knew. It was his only possession, along with his father's penknife, some clothes, and the Sanskrit dictionary.

The next morning, ready to leave, he took a handful of turmeric powder—for purity—from the kitchen and wet it down with water, just as his father's ashes had been wet down. Then he modeled a little image of the god Ganesh. He bowed his head and asked Ganesh to protect him on the journey, just as he had so often heard his father do before embarking on a pilgrimage. Then he scattered the image made of red turmeric, which, for those prayerful moments, had become the wise and compassionate Lord Ganesh. Staring at the wet lump in front of which he had just bowed, Jeffrey wondered if his prayer had been meaningless. During Father's illness, he had prayed not only to Ganesh but to Shiva and Vishnu and Shakti as well, but without success. His father had always warned him never to beg but only to worship, yet this time he had pleaded for his father's life, and the gods had not heard him. If the gods existed to hear him. What, after all, could he believe if his belief had failed him in the one thing that really counted? Still, out of habit perhaps, he had prayed to Ganesh for a safe journey.

With the suitcase in one hand and the copper urn in the other, Jeffrey left the house. He did not turn for a last glance at it, but stood under the peepul tree, squinting through its tangled limbs at the sky, recalling how Father and he had sat under it in the evenings to talk and watch the stars.

Then he walked to the bus stop. It was a long wait for the district bus bound for Trichy, but then no one ever knew when it would come rattling along, its red sides peeling and caked with dust, belching a black exhaust, too crowded for all prospective passengers to climb aboard. Fortunately the bus, when it came today, was only half full; then Jeffrey remembered it was Tuesday, which many Hindus consider inauspicious for traveling. So he found a window seat and laid his suitcase on his lap and the urn on top of it, snuggled in one arm. The bus drew off in a gnashing of gears. It commenced a lurching, swaying progress, as if it were not a single unit but a succession of small boxes linked together, somewhat like a train. Leaving the village, Jeffrey saw the cream-colored Mission School; in a first-floor classroom sat Rama, who at this hour must be struggling with math.

"Write me."

"I always will. All my life."

Jeffrey clutched the urn and gazed resolutely ahead. A few kilometers out of the village he saw a half-dozen men coming along the road, single file, dressed only in scanty loincloths, bearing pointed staffs that could be used for spears. Jeffrey knew them and waved; one, seeing him, waved back and grinned, his flat face and heavy jaw glistening in the sunlight. These men were Irulas, who lived in a forest not far away. The tribe lived by gathering roots and hunting small game. His father used to say that no people in the world were as independent as Irulas. An Irula could digest almost anything. For a feast he would catch a field mouse and cook it in rice dug up from stores buried in the ground by gerbils. Some of the local Irulas caught poisonous snakes and sold them in Madras to visiting naturalists who bought them for museums abroad. Once when Father tried to interest the Irulas in farming small vegetable plots, they only laughed, but generously repaid his kindness—by bringing him, as a gift, a five-foot banded krait, a snake whose venom matched that of a cobra. Father graciously accepted the cage with the krait in it, but next day took it into a field and released the snake. Jeffrey had never told Father about hunting vipers with Rama and selling their skins to local farmers. Father would never kill anything, not even cockroaches that often rustled across his pillow at night. Did Father now know that Jeffrey had once hunted snakes for money? "I am here." Jeffrey clutched the urn tighter. But he felt nothing against his arm except the cool metal of a copper jar. Inside there was nothing but a fine white ash.

The bus trip was long, arduous. Hour after hour he stared at the passing fields of ground nuts and black pulse. Dark-skinned farmers bent over irrigation ditches. Trails of ducks waddled through the half-submerged squares of paddy. Buffalo pulled carts loaded high with hay along the winding dirt roads that radiated off the main highway. More than once Jeffrey had the urge to leap off the bus and take one of those roads, following wherever it led, deeper into the India he loved. Lakes, streams, tiny villages nestled under coconut groves came into view, vanished, while frequently the bus halted to take on passengers who led down its narrow aisle a goat or a lamb, or held a wire cage filled with chickens for marketing.

At one stop a bewhiskered man climbed aboard, wearing Western pants and shirt, carrying an umbrella. He sat down with a heavy sigh next to Jeffrey and took a long appraising look at the suitcase, the urn, the boy's sweaty white face. After they had bounced along for a few kilometers, the man turned to Jeffrey and said in hesitant English, "What country?"

Jeffrey answered in English. "I live in India."

"Yes, yes, but coming from what country?"

"India."

The man smiled skeptically, then frowned, so in Tamil Jeffrey described the location of his village. The man only frowned more, as if displeased by the boy's knowledge of the local language.

They rode a while longer before he tapped Jeffrey's arm—rather hard. "That suitcase of yours has seen better days," he said in Tamil. "Where are you going all alone? Where is your family? Do they let you travel the roads of India by yourself?"

The questions came rapid-fire. Jeffrey stared at the man, who was wiping his face with a rumpled handkerchief; there was a purple mottling on the man's cheek, often seen in this southern country, the result of skin infection.

Jeffrey politely replied that he was going to Trichy, but volunteered nothing more.

The man stared at him. "I have never seen a foreign boy your age traveling alone on these roads. What's in there?" he asked suddenly, pointing at the copper urn. "What can you have in there so valuable as to seal it with wax?"

Jeffrey did not like the man's rude insistence. He said, "My father."

"What?"

"My father's in there."

The man's back straightened; he leaned away from Jeffrey. "What are you saying!"

"His ashes are inside."

The man got up and stood in the aisle, glaring down at Jeffrey. "You speak Tamil, but you're no Indian. Indian boys don't make fun of their elders." Compressing his lips, the man staggered in the swaying bus down the aisle and took another seat. Later, when leaving the bus, he scowled at Jeffrey and on the roadside opened his black umbrella with a vicious gesture, as if somehow the force of it would punish Jeffrey.

All through the day Jeffrey gripped the urn and watched the countryside unreel kilometer by kilometer, its hot vastness taking a grip on his mind just as he gripped the urn, until at last he fell asleep. Then abruptly he awakened, fearful of dropping the urn. The familiar landscape came into view and vanished, as if running past the window on a conveyor belt and returning: the same stream, the same paddy, the same buffalo plowing the same field, the same village huts clustered at the foot of the same hill. This was home. How could he leave it? And yet he had promised to make his destiny America. Finally the sun slipped behind a distant range of hills, its dull red the color of turmeric in the western sky. Then it became fainter and drained off like a wave receding into the ocean from a beach. He tried to keep awake as the bus continued through the night, as more people climbed aboard and then debarked, until all their faces seemed alike to him, merging together through the long, dark, hot hours into a single flow of features. And still the bus rattled on, coming after midnight into the city of Trichy. It passed near the high Rock Fort at the top of which, lit all night, was a famous temple dedicated to Ganesh. Father had taken him there on another important occasion. From its height they had gazed together at the ancient city of Trichy and beyond the city limits at the fields disappearing on the horizon in a liquid blue haze. They had both offered flowers to Ganesh on that day. And on that day his father had turned to him solemnly and said, "Lord Ganesh understands our grief, Jeffrey. I feel your mother's presence here." Thereafter his father had called him Ganesh, the name Jeffrey had carried with him to the village when they moved from Madras.

At the bus terminal Jeffrey asked for the bus to the Chola Dam. He was told by a yawning official that it would not leave until nearly daybreak. "I will call you," the man said.

So Jeffrey sat against a wall, suitcase behind him to protect it from quick hands, and with both his arms around the urn. He let his head fall awkwardly forward, but so exhausted was he that Jeffrey fell instantly asleep.

×　　　×　　　×

"You want that bus to the dam? There it is," the official said, roughly poking his shoulder. "There it is," the man repeated with a smile, when Jeffrey held the urn tighter, as if someone had tried to wrench it from him.

The official pointed to an old bus parked in the terminal. It tilted to the right, because over the years so many passengers, riding outside when inside was too crowded, had bent its undercarriage springs.

In a few minutes Jeffrey was headed for the dam. In an hour he would be there and do what was to be done. Then he'd return to Trichy and take a train for Madras and see a Mr. Lowry, who had known his father years ago. It was all in the instructions. And then—America.

But he was not thinking of the future now; the present in the round shape of a copper urn held his full attention. Jeffrey glanced at his hands; he understood if the bus ride were smooth, he'd see them trembling. Dots of light from naked bulbs in the entrance of small buildings and from candles in the doorways of mud huts lined the streets out of Trichy. The bus stopped frequently, but at this hour only a few people, going to early-morning jobs, boarded. Soon all the lights vanished, as the bus entered the countryside. This was the most difficult part of the journey—the last half-hour before he reached the dam site. Since there was no one sitting beside him, Jeffrey put the urn on the next seat and opened his suitcase. Inside were a half-dozen shirts and pants, some underwear, a comb, a pair of Western shoes, documents his father had left in the strongbox—his birth certificate, his parents' marriage certificate, passports and registrations of various kinds—and the stack of rupees secured with rubber bands, and the bronze Ganesh. Under the clothes he found his father's penknife. He put this in his pocket and closed the suitcase.

"When is the Chola Dam?" he called out in Tamil to the driver.

"I'll let you know."

There was a faint color outside the bus window now—a deep-water blue slightly distinguishable from the blackness. As the minutes passed, the blue lightened and took on a pinkish hue. When nearly a third of the sky had taken on this shade of pink, the driver called, "Here! The dam!" and stopped.

Jeffrey got out and watched the bus slowly disappear in the blue ocean of early dawn. Then he looked around. Ahead, through the gloom, was a long bridge, at this time of morning wholly deserted. He could not see across it, but he knew that on the other side was a small island, then the dam, and another channel of the great river. He knew. Because he had been here before. Because he had come with Father when a small copper urn had contained other ashes. Because together they had brought Mother here. Jeffrey had been only nine then. He had not gone to the crematory, but when Father decided that this site on the Cauvery River was the right place, Jeffrey had accompanied him. They had come at midday, but even now, five years later and in the gloom of dawn, Jeffrey could recognize everything: the broad arc of the Cauvery between heavily wooded banks and the great length of the narrow cement bridge, and a single oak standing near the entrance of the walkover. He started out, his feet slapping against the cement, making a lonely hollow sound. Overhead a crescent moon and the last few stars were visible; their light was steadily invaded from the east by a pink changing into gold. Beneath him the black water looked like a vast sheet of lead, quiet, fixed in its channel, motionless. Only his feet on the bridge made a sound—click, click, click, click—bringing him and the copper urn closer to their destination. When he reached the small island at the far end, there was enough light for him to see distinctly some bushes and trees, a small deserted kiosk, a sign both in English and in Tamil warning visitors to respect the regulations regarding public property. He remembered the sign. By the time he crossed the little expanse of island greenery to the other side, a shaft of golden light was glinting on the blue water. Beached on the riverbank were three fishing boats, their owners hunkering around a small fire, drinking tea.

Jeffrey went down to them, carrying the urn in one hand, the suitcase in the other.

One of the men, sleepy-eyed, glanced up at him. "What do we have here, a foreign kid!" he said in Tamil to the others.

"Good morning," said Jeffrey in Tamil too.

All three studied him curiously. "What country?" a fisherman said in halting English.

"This country," Jeffrey replied in Tamil.

"You," the man said, pointing at him. "What country? States?"

"I am from this country." Jeffrey tapped the earth with his foot.

The men looked at one another. "Want something?" one asked gruffly in Tamil.

"Yes. Someone to row me to the middle of the river."

"What for?"

Jeffrey thrust out the urn solemnly. "My father's ashes."

"Not me," said a fisherman, turning toward the fire.

"I will pay."

"You couldn't pay me enough for that," said another, sipping tea. "I'm not starting my day with that."

"How much will you pay?" asked the third.

"Ten rupees."

"Twenty."

"Fifteen."

"Eighteen."

"Sixteen."

"Seventeen. That's it," said the fisherman.

Jeffrey shrugged. There was no choice. "All right. Seventeen."

"You couldn't get me to do that for seventeen rupees," sneered the second fisherman, blowing on the surface of his hot tea.

"No, but you don't have five kids to feed," said the third fisherman, rising. "Come on," he waved at Jeffrey and started for the riverbank, where his old rowboat was beached. "You going to take that too?" he asked, pointing at the suitcase. "Why not leave it here with them? They'll take good care of it."

The other fishermen grinned at Jeffrey, who knew if he left the suitcase in their care, it would be gone when he returned.

"I'll take it," Jeffrey said, throwing the suitcase into the boat and climbing in after it.

The third fisherman laughed and shoved the boat free of the riverbank, then jumped in. "You're no foreigner," he said, taking the oars and starting to row.

"No, I'm not. I just look like one."

"You fooled us," the fisherman said, stroking for the river channel.

"I'm a Tamil."

"Was your mother?"

"No."

"Then, your father?"

"No," Jeffrey admitted.

The fisherman frowned and pulled hard at the oars. "You might speak Tamil, but you're a foreigner just the same. Both your mother and father were—that makes you one. There's no way around it."

Jeffrey did not respond, but sat stiffly on the thwart. The oars dipped with a plunking sound into the slowly moving river. The sun, edging above a distant line of palms, made a beady golden circle on the flat water. Dawn was swift this morning and brilliant.

Kerplunk. Kerplunk. Now the entire sun had heaved up over the horizon, its rays stretching across the water, streaking the huge dam with an orange swathe of color. The whole world seemed to have risen with the sun, taken part of its color, come alive when it did.

Jeffrey looked down at the urn between his feet. As if reading his thoughts, the boatman stopped rowing and held out his hand. "Pay me now. Before you do anything."

Taking three five-rupee notes and two singles from his pocket, Jeffrey leaned forward to count them into the extended, heavily seamed hand.

"Where exactly do you want me to go?" the fisherman then asked pleasantly.

"To the middle." Jeffrey remembered as if it were yesterday that a boatman had asked his father the same question.

Kerplunk. Kerplunk. Kerplunk.

Jeffrey squinted into the golden light at a flock of birds standing in shallow water on the far shore.

Kerplunk. Kerplunk. Kerplunk.

"How's this?" the boatman asked.

Jeffrey did not want to stop rowing. He felt that each pull of an oar prolonged his decision to carry out the act. But judging from both banks, Jeffrey knew they were indeed in the middle of the river. This was the place where his parents would join each other again.

"Stop here," he said.

The boatman put up his oars with a clunky wooden thud and yanked them out of the tholes. The boat drifted. The only sound then was the river lapping musically against the sides. Then the man turned his back and looked over the stern, away from Jeffrey.

For this gesture Jeffrey was grateful. It was easier to do what must be done without someone watching. He remembered vividly, as if it had happened only minutes ago, how his father had done with the same penknife what he was doing now—slitting the cloth lid of the urn. Jeffrey cut away the cloth entirely. His hands were not trembling. Had his father's hands trembled five years ago? It was something he could not remember; perhaps it was the only thing he could not remember. Tears filled his eyes. They weren't only for Father now, but for Mother too. His parents had come to the same place again, at last.

Jeffrey cleared his throat, reached down and gripped the copper urn with both hands and held it over the gunwale. He stared at the water flowing away from the side of the boat, little bubbles rising and vanishing. He said, "River Cauvery, take back what belongs to rivers. Take back what is yours." He remembered his father's words exactly and now used them for his father. Then he tilted the jar and watched the whitish ashes slide with a feathery motion from the jar's mouth into the water. For a few moments the ashes floated, then, becoming heavy, were drawn down into the depths of the Cauvery. Jeffrey shook the jar until all the ashes had fallen into the water. What had Father done with the other jar? Befuddled a moment, Jeffrey couldn't remember. Reaching down, he filled this jar with enough water to sink it. The shining copper, dazzling in the light, disappeared with a bubbling gurgle.

It was done. What did he feel? Relief. He had brought the ashes to this place safely. A sense of accomplishment too. He had done his duty as a son. And then a terrific rush of emptiness. He searched over the gunwale for a final trace of ash in the water, but his eyes met only a vast perpetual movement of the river. Nothing else. Here there was not even ashes, not even the urn that had carried them. Nothing here.

"Tell me when you're finished," said the boatman, still facing away.

"I'm done now."

The boatman turned and raised his eyebrows in surprise. "Where's that jar? Did you throw it in too? That's a waste, boy! I'd have used it just fine."

But Jeffrey scarcely heard him. His attention was abruptly fixed on the opposite bank, where birds had gathered at the shore or were twittering among the overhanging limbs of trees. There was a sense of quickening in the air, as if something was going to happen. Jeffrey

61

leaned forward, gazing steadily at the birds—white and pink and brown and red patches of color against the golden shore.

Words entered his mind: "I am here."

And other words: "We are here!"

And then suddenly the egrets, terns, and herons flapped heavily into the golden morning, their broad wings catching the wind and moving rapidly against the background of a sky shimmering in sunlight.

"We are here."

Shading his eyes, Jeffrey squinted at the rising birds until losing them in the sun's rays. He sat back and looked at the man pulling the oars. "I'm sorry. I shouldn't have wasted that jar." He remembered that Father had given the other jar to the first person who came along when they reached shore five years ago. Father had given it away for someone to use. It was only a jar; it was nothing to fear or treasure. And what had been in it was part of the water, mingling with the elements in midcurrent. "I should have given that jar to you," he told the boatman, who nodded with a frown.

Because that's not where Father was, where they both were.

"We are here. We are everywhere."

He followed the soaring, pulsing rhythm of another flock of birds rising from the riverbank. Everywhere. "We are here and everywhere."

Part 2

The idea of America took hold of him thousands of feet above ground, an hour away from the airport where his aunt would be waiting. So much had happened to Jeffrey in the last few weeks that the idea of America had remained no more than that—a remote idea. Staying with Mr. Lowry in Madras, he had been caught up in the labyrinthine details of departure. And the transcontinental flight, a new and bewildering experience, had occupied his mind to the exclusion of other thoughts. Then the landing at a New York airport, where he changed planes, had given him no sense of place; it had been an impersonal arena, filled with voices, anxious faces, hurrying feet.

Now, in less than an hour, he must face a strange truth: he was an American. Although his parents had come from the States, they had rarely spoken of it. Father, especially, seemed to have put aside all recollections of his earlier life. Each mile traveled with the Swami through India had increased the distance between Father and the past. Father had put his memories of America inside a balloon of the mind, cut the string, let it sail away, effortlessly. And the result? Jeffrey knew very little about his own country—or rather the country that was supposed to be his.

He stared from the plane window at a cloudless sky. It must be many degrees below zero beyond the pane of glass, yet for him such a brilliant canopy of blue meant the scorching midday heat of south India. Glancing at the wristwatch of the man beside him, Jeffrey realized with mounting excitement that within an hour he would step into a new world. Yet with the excitement he felt another and perhaps stronger emotion: the desire to turn back, go home, home to India, to the south, to his own village, to his tiny house and stuffy little room.

He had come this far not by his own choice, but because of a promise. He understood, of course, why Father had demanded it of him. After the funeral it had become painfully clear that his place was no longer in the village. Yet nothing would erase his conviction that India was his true home. Father had said, "Try America, then if you wish, return to India." What stuck in Jeffrey's mind was the last phrase: "Return to India." Once his obligation had been fulfilled—to try America—he meant to go back, even if the villagers did not feel he belonged.

As minutes passed and the plane began its descent, he felt an overpowering rush of excitement that swept away his reluctance to undergo this American experience. Below, coming into view, was the earth: large flat squares of it, set off from one another by pencil-thin lines that soon became wire fences. The patches were white. They startled Jeffrey, who had expected greenery or at least the dusty brown earth of summer drought, even though he knew it was still winter here. The white meant snow. Out of it rose spindly gray trees and red farmhouses scattered across the vast frozen plain. Father in his teens had been used to this white landscape of winter. The grown man who had trudged the steamy paths of India had also trudged through snow. Father had been two men.

Over a loudspeaker the stewardess was talking. It was not easy for Jeffrey to decipher every word, because she spoke English in an accent foreign to him: American! The man beside Jeffrey tapped his arm. "Fasten your seat belt."

They were landing.

✕   ✕   ✕

The woman rushing toward him, arms outspread, was his aunt. He knew it from the craggy features of her face, from the light blue eyes so like his father's. She hugged him hard before pulling back to get a good look at him. Jeffrey glanced self-consciously around. What would people think of such a public display? But no one seemed to notice. Perhaps in America it was all right to do such a thing. Aunt Betty, her eyes level with his, gave him a broad smile.

"You're just like your father was at your age!"

She didn't wait for a response, but kept talking, while leading him out of the crowd with her hand on his elbow. She was talking about the very cold weather for this time of year—it should be warmer—and how the arrival of the flight was delayed almost fifteen minutes, which

65

had given her a moment of worry. She said other things too, rapidly, so Jeffrey could not pick everything out of the stream of words. His aunt was thin—he could see this though she wore a full-length winter coat—and looked maybe ten years older than Father. Her voice had a musical sound to it, even though she was nervous, and she smiled a lot.

Jeffrey was surprised that he liked her immediately.

It occurred to him that somewhere in the back of his mind during the latter part of the flight, he had created the image of a strict, gloomy woman, somewhat like the woman in a Dickens novel that the Mission School class had been reading. The image didn't fit his aunt, and he felt relieved.

They reached the baggage area to wait for the flight luggage to be unloaded. When Jeffrey picked up his suitcase, Aunt Betty asked how many bags he had brought.

"Only this one."

For an instant she frowned, as if contemplating the fact that her nephew had arrived with almost nothing. "I always say it's better to travel light," she remarked then with a smile. "Do you have a warmer jacket in the suitcase?"

"No, ma'am."

Aunt Betty shook her head. "That cotton jacket isn't near warm enough in this weather."

In a Madras store Mr. Lowry had purchased it for Jeffrey; in 105 degree heat, it had seemed much too warm.

"Tomorrow we'll get you a warm coat." As they headed for the entrance of the small terminal, Aunt Betty continued talking: she had hired a car today because it wouldn't do for him to ride a bus back to town on his arrival; so it was a little extravagance they could afford; she had sold her own car last year because a widow doesn't go out much anyway. She went on, while Jeffrey stared through the terminal window at the airport bus she had mentioned: big, streamlined, shiny, with high tinted windows, and enormous tires. Another image flashed through his mind: an old bus coughing smoke, tilting to one side, while on the suitcase across his lap rested a copper urn.

On impulse Aunt Betty abruptly halted and gripped Jeffrey by the shoulders. "I have dreamed and dreamed of this day for years, Jeffrey. How I have hoped for you to come here! Only—" She paused and let her hands fall. "I never thought it would be under these circumstances. But don't talk about it," she added quickly, as if Jeffrey had been talking. "Don't say a word till you've had the chance to settle in."

"I won't talk about my father's death, ma'am, till you are ready," Jeffrey said. They were the most words he had yet spoken.

His aunt raised her eyebrows and laughed nervously. "Why, boy, you have an English accent. But you would, wouldn't you. You would! Oh, I'm so glad you're here at last! At home. *Your* home. Wait till I get the car." The words spilled out so fast that Jeffrey's Indian ear could not quite gather them all in. He watched her rush into the parking lot. A blast of wintry air from the opened door met Jeffrey and surprised him; he had never experienced a temperature below 60 degrees. Cold air was cold! He hunched into his cotton jacket and watched the thin figure of his aunt move swiftly across the windswept lot to a car. Soon the driver pulled the car up to the airport entrance, his aunt gesturing briskly from the backseat.

Jeffrey stepped out into the midwestern cold. He was

not sure that he liked it. What he hadn't expected was a kind of burning sensation on his cheeks. It was the cold that did this all right, although for a moment it felt hot like noontime in a south Indian field.

When he was in the car, Aunt Betty sighed and patted his hand. "We travel in style today, but tomorrow it won't be like that. Tomorrow we go back to buses!" She explained that their town was twenty miles to the west; this was the closest city with an airport. Their town was surrounded by farmland and many of its citizens were retired farmers. She talked on, while Jeffrey took quick glances at the passing countryside: the hedged white fields, the cylindrical gray silos, the red farmhouses. A cloud bank had descended suddenly from the north, and before the car had gone a few miles, snowflakes began to dance in front of the windshield. Because of them, Jeffrey was unable to concentrate on his aunt's flow of words. Snow—he watched the white fluffs scooting and rocking in the air currents. It was a strange world to him: it was misty, the distance seeming to fold back on itself in layers, the look of the land metallic and silent. Around him was not the soft, cozy gray of a monsoon sky, but something different. He felt as though the atmosphere backed away from the car, forever receding. It did not envelop you like the atmosphere of a monsoon; it was always moving away, eluding you. These thoughts were in his mind as Aunt Betty continued to talk about— about what? Food? It seemed to be about food.

Jeffrey heard himself say, "That sounds okay."

Aunt Betty laughed. "Okay? Do you use that word in India?"

"Yes, like that, ma'am. Even people who cannot speak English."

"Are there many who can't?"

"Most cannot in south India."

"Then how do you speak to them?"

"In their language."

Aunt Betty smiled in acknowledgment of her ignorance. "I keep forgetting you come from somewhere else, Jeffrey. The fact is, you *look* so much like one of us! So much like your father." On this last remark her voice wavered and seemed to fail her. Jeffrey looked away. He understood that all of her talk came of nervousness, grief, and confusion. He had gone through Father's death, whereas she had yet to do so. Maybe in a way she was doing it now, with him beside her in the black car moving through the grim winter light.

✗   ✗   ✗

On first seeing the rambling three-story clapboard house, he thought of Rama's house in the village. Both were big, set back at the far end of a broad lawn. In the rapidly falling snow that slanted obliquely across the shuttered windows and porch, the slate gray house seemed immense and, unlike Rama's house, mysterious. The snow was like a veil through which the tall gabled structure emerged from a slightly rolling ascent, dotted with bushes and a skeletal oak, its trunk gnarled and snow-coated where the wind struck it with flurries. He hunched deeply into his thin jacket, carrying his suitcase while Aunt Betty led the way up the walk, talking ceaselessly: "That bush nearly died last autumn, but a man here in town can do wonders if you get him to doctor a plant in time."

Jeffrey glanced around in wonder at the stark mouse-colored bushes vanishing slowly under layers of white.

He sensed the muted quality of the air, as if a huge invisible hand had come down and held the earth lightly in the tent of its fingers. He gazed up at the porch rising above him, as they negotiated the slippery incline to the front steps. Looking up, up, up, he saw against the watery atmosphere of the winter sky an old black weather vane, a metal rooster standing against the wind that blew steadily, soundlessly, from the north.

"We are home," said Aunt Betty with a sigh.

Home? This white, silent winter place?

Once inside the house, Jeffrey followed her example and stomped his snowy shoes hard on the doormat.

"I left a fire going, so we could have it when we got home. I hope it hasn't gone out altogether," Aunt Betty was saying breathlessly. Hanging her coat on a hook, she flung open a set of double doors and went into a large parlor. Jeffrey removed his jacket too, shivering a little, and went inside, where his aunt was already bending at a fireplace, stirring the coals with an iron poker. Jeffrey scanned the large musty parlor, dimly lit by the bleak light of a snowy afternoon. The furniture was large, dark, bulky. The lamps of colored glass had tassels of white crystal hanging from their shades. The dingy wallpaper had small patterns of triangular designs. It was a far cry from the plain green plaster walls of his village home—of nearly every village home. Over the fireplace hung two large portraits: one of a stiff-backed, white-haired, fierce-looking old man who wore a black tie and black jacket; the other of a solemn, bespectacled, white-haired old woman who wore a plain print dress with a high collar. Jeffrey stared at them. They looked uncomfortable, posed so rigidly, but on a second look they didn't seem so forbidding—they had nice eyes. The old man possessed huge hands.

With a snapping sound a new log caught fire from the coals and within a few minutes, while Aunt Betty kept up a running commentary on the fire's progress, hearty flames leapt briskly toward the chimney flue.

Fire.

The last fire Jeffrey had seen had eaten the body of his father. Inside the blaze had been the oblong bundle that abruptly sat erect.

"Jeffrey?"

His aunt had asked him something. He turned, quizzically.

"Are you hungry?" she repeated.

"Yes, ma'am."

Aunt Betty shook her head with a smile. "Been so long since I heard a young person say ma'am." She jabbed at the fire with the poker. "Nothing like a fire on a day like this. Makes you cozy, doesn't it." Turning, she looked steadily at him. Her lips were trembling. "Was it—difficult for your father?"

"Dad never complained."

"So you called him 'Dad.' " The idea seemed to please her. "No, he wouldn't complain. Not Warren." Again she stared hard at Jeffrey. "May I ask you something?" Again her lips trembled. "Does he have a marker?"

"Ma'am?"

"A marker, a cross on his grave."

"No, ma'am." In answer to his aunt's frown, Jeffrey added, "He was cremated. In our village, people are."

"Ah!" She looked surprised. "Cremated." She pursed her lips thoughtfully. "Well, it's done here too—for some.

71

Your family, most of it—at least on your father's side—is buried not ten minutes' drive from this house." Again her lips trembled. "But his ashes? Are they in an urn somewhere?"

"I took them to a sacred river."

"A sacred river?"

"I poured his ashes into the Cauvery River. That's where he took Mother's."

Aunt Betty nodded, her eyes filling with tears. "I see. The two of them there." She cleared her throat. "Yes, well, I'm going to show you your room and then see about dinner. I don't know about you, but I'm starving!"

Halfway up the bare-wood, creaking stairway, Aunt Betty halted and said musingly, "A *sacred* river?"

"Yes, ma'am."

For the first time since Jeffrey had met his aunt, she really fell silent. There was a long narrow hall at the end of which she turned a doorknob and stood back to let him enter.

"Go on," she urged with a smile. "It's your room."

It wasn't big, although twice the size of his room in the village. There was a bed that looked soft and comfortable with a thick quilt on it. The desk in front of the window was of dark solid wood and seemed heavy, sturdy, a thing that had stood there ever since the house had been built.

"Your father's desk," Aunt Betty said behind him.

A photograph sat on it. As Jeffrey bent to look at a boy who must have been about his own age when the snapshot was taken, his aunt said, "Your father."

Jeffrey leaned closer for a better look.

"See the resemblance? I wasn't fooling when I said at the airport you looked like him!"

It was true. Although his own face was not quite so sharp featured—his cheekbones were broad like his mother's—yet there he was: his own face smiling out of a picture and his body wearing clothes that he had never worn, a leather jacket, corduroy pants, lumberjack boots.

"This was your father's room. Now it's yours."

Jeffrey turned to see her leaving.

"You wash up," she said, "while I get dinner ready."

He had not been alone for a moment since leaving Mr. Lowry's house in Madras for the airport. He heard ticking. On a little table was a bedside clock, its old pendulum moving from side to side. It must be very old. Maybe it had once belonged to the stern-looking old man in the portrait above the downstairs fireplace. Was that his grandfather—or great-grandfather? There were certificates on the walls of this room: he saw his father's name on them. They were certificates, awards, and diplomas coming out of his father's past. Father had earned them, just as Father had earned respect by walking with the Swami across the length and breadth of India. But it was too bad that Father had not told him something about this world here, because now he was living in it too.

Jeffrey sat on the bed; it felt as good as it looked. Outside the window more snow was falling, falling steadily and gently, as the light faded, withdrawing itself from the intricate bare limbs of a tree just beyond the pane of glass. The only sound was the clock ticking. The walls were papered with an overall blue pattern of some people sitting under a tree beside a stream and some birds flying overhead. The people were repeated up and down the wall, and the birds flew in endlessly similar formations.

The wallpaper and falling snow gave him a sense of peace and drowsiness, so he leaned back until lying flat on the bed. His bed. In another minute Jeffrey might have fallen asleep had he not heard Aunt Betty calling from downstairs.

His first dinner in America awaited Jeffrey Moore.

✖   ✖   ✖

What he saw, sitting on the dining table laid with a white cloth, appalled him: a big, golden brown turkey, the juices seeping through the split skin of its breast.

What he felt must have shown on his face, because Aunt Betty's smile turned abruptly to a frown of alarm. "Is something wrong?"

"No, nothing, ma'am. It all is looking good." He sat down and noticed a heaping pile of mashed potatoes in a dish, some slices of carrots in another. Then he stared at the big turkey.

"Will you carve?" his aunt asked, offering him a carving knife and fork.

"No, thank you, aunty. I don't know how."

"Let me do it, then." She began working on the turkey, glancing curiously at him now and then, where he sat at rigid attention. "You called me aunty. Is that what you do in India?"

He didn't understand the question, so he gave her a puzzled look.

"In India, you say aunty?"

"Yes, ma'am."

"I see. In America, boys your age usually say aunt. Nothing wrong with aunty," she said with a shrug, working through the tendons of a turkey leg and skillfully parting it from the carcass. "Except here I suspect boys

74

your age wouldn't understand your calling me aunty."

Jeffrey nodded, grateful for her tact. She was trying hard to teach him something without making him look foolish. And she was doing everything she could to make him feel at home. Only, when he stared at the huge leg of turkey, which she slid off the fork onto his plate, Jeffrey felt like running.

"Anything wrong?" she asked. "You prefer white meat?"

He shook his head.

"Take some potatoes and carrots. I hope you like it," she added anxiously. "I'd have made something special, like Swiss steak, only there just wasn't time."

"I like potatoes and carrots very much, thank you, aunt." Jeffrey spooned liberal helpings onto his plate, but kept them separate from the turkey meat.

"Here is gravy," Aunt Betty said, thrusting a gravy boat at him.

After a moment of hesitation, he took it from her hand. "Is this sauce being made from the bird?" he asked.

She laughed. "Of course it is! I don't use canned gravy or any of that frozen stuff. Best turkey you can get in this town. From Ralston's Grocery. He has the best butcher—why, Mr. Ralston took care of your grandparents."

Jeffrey was holding the gravy boat above his plate with both hands. "This sauce is from meat?"

She was looking hard at him. "Jeffrey. Something *is* wrong."

He handed back the gravy boat. "Yes, ma'am."

"Then tell me, boy."

"I am not eating meat."

Aunt Betty laid down her fork and finished chewing

the piece of turkey in her mouth. Then she said, "Are you some kind of a vegetarian, Jeffrey?"

He nodded, looking down at his plate. "I am not taking meat or eggs or food cooked in animal fat, Aunt Betty."

"Is this your father's teaching?"

"Yes, ma'am."

"When did you become a vegetarian?"

"When I was born."

"Good Lord."

"I have never taken meat. If I know there is meat or eggs in something, I am not taking."

Aunt Betty stopped chewing. "You poor child!"

"No, it's okay," he said reassuringly.

"But you're a healthy, growing boy!"

"No, it's okay. I am used to it, aunt. It's my habit."

She leaned toward him. "You do this from some conviction?"

"My parents were not taking meat, so I am not either."

"It was their belief?"

Jeffrey nodded.

She had lifted her fork with some potatoes on it, but put it down again. "Was their belief *religious*?"

Jeffrey nodded.

"Boy, are you a Christian?"

"No, ma'am."

"Warren raised you this way?"

"Yes, ma'am. Both my parents were Hindus."

"Hindus," Aunt Betty repeated, having stopped eating altogether. "They worshiped some kind of idol?"

"Yes, ma'am. More than one. They were also praying to Jesus Christ and Allah. Father said the Lord has different forms but one reality."

76

"Well, I must say that sounds like Warren—deep," Aunt Betty observed with a sigh and picked up her fork again. "Jeffrey," she said after a long silence, "are you a Hindu?"

"I was."

"Are you now?"

Jeffrey shook his head. "I don't know what I am being, aunt."

"I see," she replied quietly. "You have been through a lot."

There was another silence, after which she said, "But whatever you are—Hindu or Christian or whatever—you won't eat meat."

"It has not been my habit, aunt."

"All right then, you'll eat the way you want to. Only I never did cook vegetarian before, so you'll have to help me. Can you do that?"

"Yes, ma'am. I thank you."

"A vegetarian," his aunt mused. Then giving him a broad smile, she said, "I guess we never get too old to learn new things."

"Thank you," he said, digging into the gravyless potatoes. "These potatoes are okay," he said, eating them. "Very good. Like that."

"I'm glad you think they're okay. Here, let me get that off your plate." She reached over with her fork and speared the huge turkey leg.

"Carrots are good too," he said with his mouth full.

"Eat all you want." For a thoughtful moment she studied the turkey leg, now on her own plate, then, with a sigh of decision, cut off a healthy slice and ate it.

×　　　×　　　×

For the next few days Jeffrey spent most of his time becoming acquainted with the house. It was like a person, like someone in the family he must get to know. He wandered from room to room, getting a feel for the winter sunshine streaming through the windows and falling upon curtains, tables, carpets. He heard the sounds of different clocks ticking. Some rooms smelled musty, since they were not used. Others smelled of fresh linen and disinfectant—like his own and his aunt's rooms. Aunt Betty spent most of her time cleaning the large house or going downtown on the bus. He went with her a couple of times, once to buy a warm zippered jacket and once to the grocery. He stood in the middle of a supermarket aisle and gawked at the rows of canned goods, at the frozen food sections, at the bewildering variety of boxed products. In his village the shopping was done in tiny stalls or from vegetables spread out on mats on the ground or set in wooden carts. At the bus stand downtown he surveyed the large shops surrounding the square. All the streets were paved. Every street had its own sidewalk for pedestrians, and houses were set back from it. Cars drove everywhere—not small Indian Ambassadors, but long, powerful cars, and trucks big enough to hold two or three Indian varieties. And there was not a single cow or goat strolling down the middle of a road.

But his main interest continued to be the house and the life that had occupied it for the last century. At dinner—his aunt cooked herself a portion of meat to go along with the vegetables, his own helpings liberally spiced with black pepper—Jeffrey listened intently to stories about the Family Moore. His great-grandfather, the stern man domineering the parlor from above the fireplace, had built this house in time spared from the full practice of law. Once, after dinner, Aunt Betty took Jeffrey upstairs, unlocked a room with one of the myriad keys on a long chain, and took him inside. The room was cold, damp, airless. She turned on the light and pointed to a large bed with a multicolored quilt and a wooden canopy over it draped with a white lace curtain.

"Your father was born right in this bed, Jeffrey," she told him, touching his shoulder. "So was I. Your great-grandparents both died in this bed. So did your grandmother. Your grandfather wanted to go here, but he died in the hospital. I have regretted not getting him back home, where he belonged, where his wife, my mother, went when it was time, where his parents went too."

Jeffrey looked at her. Aunt Betty stared so hard at the bed that he wondered if she could see people lying in it.

For a flashing moment he saw fire rising from the bed, flames crackling, a figure jerking upright from the quilt.

"You see?" Aunt Betty said with a wan smile. "This house has memories. Now it is yours too, Jeffrey."

One afternoon she gave him a tour of the unoccupied third floor, where there were four rooms, all of them used for storage now. His great-grandparents had had six children, therefore a reason for building such a large house. Only one of their children, however—Jeffrey's grandfather—had remained in this town, the rest having wandered across the face of the earth.

"It was the same restless spirit your father had," observed Aunt Betty.

Jeffrey strolled through each room, and although they were filled with the mustiness of disuse, he did not feel they were impersonal. Presences filled them. He would not have been surprised if someone had abruptly emerged from one of the closed bathrooms or, for that matter, from a closet—and wearing clothes of a century ago. Each room was individualized by a photograph or an object. One of his great-uncles had a collection of guns in a glass cabinet that he had brought home after forty years in Africa. One of his great-aunts had collected pewter plates from all corners of the world. This house was peopled in such a way that Jeffrey did not seem lonely in it with only his aunt for company. Memories drifted here in the halls, in the rooms: soundless cries of other children, feet scurrying down the gleaming corridors that his aunt now kept polished. Not that Jeffrey felt threatened by this house. He simply knew that it had been thoroughly lived in and some of its life had remained within the walls, giving the house a sense of continuous habitation. In a way it was a village of his own creation now, peopled by his unfamiliar ancestors, who were there to bar from his path any feeling of loneliness that might come along.

The weather became abruptly mild on his fourth day in town. Snow, gleaming in the sunlight, began to melt, to draw away from the base of tree and bush, to recede and shrivel upon the ground like white balloons emptied of air. He went outside and strolled in the yard. Within the sunshine he was warm, but standing in the lee of the house in blue shadow, he felt the thrill of cold on his face and hands. He wished that Rama might be here to share the sensation of such cold. Looking up at the weather vane, he saw the icy clouds scud past the large oblong of land occupied by the house. His house. *His* house? Aunt Betty told him it belonged to him now—

and he to it. Just as Rama belonged to a large family house in the village. He could recall now the stab of envy felt whenever Rama or others in that family had spoken of generations past with such pride and feeling. But how, Jeffrey wondered, could you belong to something that was so unfamiliar to you? Yet he did; he belonged to this house in a strange country in the middle of winter, with snow at his feet. Inside the house, working in the kitchen, a woman would tell him again and again that this was his place, his heritage.

By the end of his first week in town, strolling in the muddy yard now bereft of snow, Jeffrey experienced a new feeling, one that he had never known before: what surrounded him was wholly his and he was its—each tree, bush, hallway, and table had the mark of his life. Even though he had always felt that he belonged to the village, it was clear now that he had always suspected it might not be true: his blond hair, his blue eyes, his fair skin had denied him a final sense of comfort. Yet did he truly belong here? Yes, he did. And he did not. Because beyond the front gate lay a cement sidewalk leading outward into a world totally strange to him. Until he was familiar with this town, the new feeling would remain in part counterfeit, suspect, no deeper perhaps than his sense of belonging to the village had once been.

✳　　✳　　✳

On his eighth day in America he went to the local school with his aunt. They spoke to the principal, who agreed to let Jeffrey enter the term late on the basis of an examination. That afternoon in the principal's office, he took a test that lasted an hour. After waiting another hour, his aunt seated gravely beside him, Jeffrey learned

81

that he could join the class for his own age group, although, understandably, he had done poorly in history. His writing was up to the minimum standard and he had scored well in math.

Aunt Betty was pleased as they walked down the school corridor, empty now that classes were in session. "I wish you could have seen your father in school," she said. "Razor sharp. But inclined to take things too lightly. Not that you could actually call him lazy—"

Jeffrey glanced shyly at three boys coming along the hall. They were a head taller than he, with broad shoulders and long hair.

"He just never cared much about excelling. That way in college too. Even though his professors *told* him and *told* him of his potential. Nearly broke his father's—your grandfather's—heart. But then Warren had a strong will, no matter how easygoing he seemed on the surface."

More boys. Also tall. And the girls were tall too. Jeffrey had been accustomed to the short, thin, slightly built people of south India, where, if anything, he had seemed big for his age.

Was he actually small? He found out the next day, when he joined the class, that among his own people he was. He went to school alone, taking the bus by himself, although Aunt Betty wanted to take him his first day. But she did not insist when he was firm about going alone. Aunt Betty had a way of smiling and saying "Do what you think you should" that made him feel easy with her.

There were more than twenty-five in his class, and the teacher introduced him as "Jeffrey Moore from India." Some of the students regarded him curiously; a few even crowded around after class to ask him where he had lived. But the long, unpronounceable name of his village was too much for them, so they shrugged and left him in the hall. Thereafter he walked alone, and between classes in the hallways he was buffeted like everyone else. What distinguished him from them was his hesitancy, his loneliness. But this was all right with him. It was better to start slowly with these strange new people whose loud voices, rough movements, and sheer ebullience were like nothing he had known in the village, where the heat held even the young, at least at midday, to a slow, energy-conserving pace, and where custom forbade loud laughter and shouting. It would not be easy either to get accustomed to the classrooms with steam knocking in the pipes and a condensation of moisture on the cold windows, so that everyone inside the classroom was peculiarly separated from the outside world. He had never been in a classroom that had a glass window. During a monsoon storm, perhaps the shutters would be closed; otherwise, he had always listened to teachers explaining and students reciting while, nearby, perhaps a crow tilted on a branch and regarded him with a critical black eye, or a green snake twined itself around a purple-blossomed bush. Moreover, he didn't mind being alone until he could understand what was happening: the assignments, the unfamiliar procedures, the relaxed classroom manners, the informality of teachers. And what shocked him was boys and girls holding hands between classes. In the village it was common practice for boys to hold hands with boys, girls with girls, but never otherwise! What did the teachers here think of a girl and a boy strolling down the corridor, their fingers entwined?

With each passing day, however, he learned more about the school and what was expected of him. Gently

83

a teacher explained that it was quite unnecessary for him to jump to attention when called on. He also learned that "a flowery" style of writing reports was not acceptable. His teacher wrote in large script across the top of his paper: "Say it plainly and clearly!" She did not know, of course, that if he had failed to call Shakespeare "the great bard and master of the ages" and the plays "masterpieces beyond compare," his teacher in the village school would not have believed he possessed sufficient appreciation of the English playwright. On an American history test Jeffrey failed abysmally, but to his relief—and gratitude—a teacher told him after class, "Take it easy; this is all new to you."

At lunch each day he got into the cafeteria line with the rest of the students. The hall was crowded, boisterous, in vertiginous motion. He felt small among the boys, even among those his own age, who were not only taller but heavier. Lunch was a difficult time for Jeffrey. Almost every day a new server stood behind the food counter. These student helpers didn't seem to understand what he meant by "not taking," when he pulled his tray back from the hefty hamburger ready to be plopped on his plate. He always got a puzzled look. Sometimes he would get a remark too: "Nothing wrong with this burger!" Or: "Hey, it's not going to bite you!"

And at the dessert section, whenever he tried to verify the composition of something, he usually got a quizzical look for an answer.

"Making with eggs?" he would ask, pointing to a dish.

"Yeah, sure. With eggs." And the dish would be thrust at him.

"No, no!" And he'd pull back his tray, often to a puzzled giggle or a contemptuous frown.

One day, when he sat down at a table in the cafeteria, two boys from his class came along. "How about sitting with you?"

Jeffrey nodded shyly.

He knew who the boys were. The very tall one was a basketball player whom Jeffrey had seen play on his first visit to the gym. Tom Carrington was by far the tallest of the fourteen-year-olds; indeed, he was among the tallest boys in the school. Although Jeffrey didn't understand the fine points of basketball, he could see in Tom Carrington's handling of the ball a great flair, a natural grace. Jeffrey was sorry that the season had already finished, that he would not have a chance to watch any games.

The other boy, shorter, but also a basketball player, was staring at something. Jeffrey looked down at his own plate, because it seemed to be what had caught Phil Booker's attention. What was wrong with his plate?

"Why don't you have some *food*?" Phil asked, frowning, digging into one of three hamburgers piled on his own plate.

"I'm having," said Jeffrey.

"What he means is," said Tom Carrington, "some meat. It will warm you up. You sure look cold all the time."

And it was true that Jeffrey felt cold much of the time. Last week the gym had been closed for repair, so physical education period was held outside. Most of the boys threw footballs around or jogged. Jeffrey had stood each period at the edge of the track, hopping from one foot to the other, hands thrust in his pockets, trying to keep warm.

"Have one of mine," Tom said abruptly and shoved his own plate of burgers forward.

"No, no, thank you. I'm not taking."

"What are you, one of those health freaks?" asked Phil with his mouth full of food.

"Healthy freaks?" Jeffrey repeated.

"You know, eating wheat germ, seeds, and organic stuff. Don't people do that over in India?"

"No, no, no," Jeffrey replied quickly, lifting a forkful of gravyless vegetables. "I am not a healthy freak. I am just not taking meat."

"So you're a vegetarian," concluded Tom.

Jeffrey nodded with a smile.

"Sure. Like I just said—a health freak," said Phil, dumping catsup on his hamburgers.

"Is everyone in India a vegetarian?" asked Tom, showing interest.

"Some are, some not."

"From what I heard of India," said Phil, "the people are so poor, they'll eat anything they can get." He turned to Tom. "That senior—what's-his-name—he's one of those vegetarians."

"Who?" Tom asked.

"What's-his-name. You know. The thin, little guy about his size." Phil jabbed his fork at Jeffrey. "Wears glasses?"

"Debates?"

"That's him. A health freak," said Phil happily and jabbed his fork again at Jeffrey. "Like you."

"Nothing wrong with being a health freak," argued Tom.

"No? My father says it's a fad."

"Listen," said Tom, "if I could raise my free-throw percentage five points, I'd eat dry leaves."

At this point Jeffrey Moore belched loudly. He was

86

wondering if these boys would like him better if he ate meat. Was it necessary in America to eat meat if you wanted friends? He didn't feel Tom Carrington took that attitude, but he wasn't sure about Phil Booker. He belched again, astonished to see a look of disgust on the faces opposite him.

"Not taking meat is my habit," he said in explanation. But apparently the boys wouldn't tolerate such a habit, because both of them were glaring at him. Exchanging glances, they got up and without a word moved to another table. What had he done? Refused meat. How could he eat something that almost everyone in his village avoided, even abhorred? Vegetarianism a fad? Then it was a fad that had lasted a thousand years in India. He watched the two boys working away at their hamburgers, now and then giving him a glance. They were leaning toward each other, saying something. It was about him, because then they gave him a scornful look. Living in America is not going to be easy, he thought. Few people would be as tolerant as his aunt.

At dinner that night he told his aunt of the incident.

Frankly puzzled, Aunt Betty screwed up her face and said, "I don't understand it, Jeffrey. I can't believe boys your age would get up a head of steam simply because you don't eat meat. Oh, maybe they might kid you a little—but get up and move to another table?" She shook her head in bewilderment.

Then the next night, Aunt Betty frowned hard at him, during dinner. "Jeffrey! What do you *say*!"

"Ma'am?"

"Do you know what you just did?"

"Ma'am?"

"What you did just *now*!"

Jeffrey considered his actions of the last few minutes, then grinned uncertainly. "I have just been taking food, aunt."

"As well as belching! You sat there and about belched in my *face,* without saying a word, 'pardon,' or anything!"

Had he belched? Jeffrey couldn't remember. What was his aunt so upset about? She looked just like the boys in the cafeteria yesterday: disgusted.

He smiled timidly.

"Jeffrey, have you any idea what I am talking about?"

"No, ma'am."

"Have you done this at school—in the cafeteria?"

"Done what, aunt?"

"Belched, as you just did here."

He shrugged. "Maybe I did. I am sorry for not remembering."

"Maybe you did while eating lunch with those two boys."

Jeffrey nodded thoughtfully. "Maybe I did."

Aunt Betty, having glared at him, slowly relaxed and leaned forward. "See here, boy, belching isn't done here in public like that. Kids may not be brought up with yesterday's strictness, but they are still taught not to belch, or if they do, at least to keep their mouths closed and certainly to pardon themselves. My goodness. Don't you pardon yourself where you come from?"

"No, ma'am."

"But didn't your father teach you anyway?"

"Dad and I took food like Indians." Jeffrey lifted his right hand and plunged it into the middle of the plate, screwing his fingertips around a gob of potatoes and lifting it to his mouth. Having eaten the morsel, he wiped his fingers and sat back solemnly. "Like that. Only with green chilis in it. Spicy food is making you belch, so you belch. No one says anything. It's okay."

His aunt shook her head sadly. "Just the same, Warren should have taught you better."

"Dad was busy with other things."

Sensing the defensiveness in his voice, Aunt Betty cleared her throat and said, "Well, now you know how it is done in our town—in *your* town—Jeffrey."

"Yes, ma'am. I think I do."

"Too bad there isn't a way to have your classmates understand the world you come from."

"Maybe someday they will."

Aunt Betty smiled. "That's the spirit. Patience and hope. It's what your grandfather used to say: always count on patience and hope."

The way Aunt Betty talked to him made Jeffrey feel at ease again. From where he sat, he could see above the mantelpiece the fine round head, white hair, and steady eyes of his great-grandfather who had built this house with two powerful hands. That night, snug in bed while a cold wind beat against the windowpane, Jeffrey thought of the stern old man and the other one staring from another portrait in the upstairs hallway—his grandfather—and once again he watched the ashes of his father disappear into the gentle current of the Cauvery River. It seemed as if three men crowded around his bed and bid him good night, good night, good night, to the ticking rhythm of the bedside clock.

✗   ✗   ✗

The school had reopened the gym, so his physical education class met for a period at the swimming pool.

After showering, the class of fifteen boys ran to poolside, jumped or dove in, while the instructor, a beefy man with a whistle around his neck, stood glaring at each one. Jeffrey watched the boys swimming. Few swam as poorly as he did, because like other boys in the village he had learned on his own. He, Rama, and three others had merely gone to a lake, stood in water up to their necks, then struck out for the shore, trying to get there any way they could. In this manner they had all learned to swim, but not like these Americans with their smoothly coordinated motion of arms and legs. He felt awkward when he jumped in and flailed out for the opposite side.

At the sound of the whistle, everyone climbed from the pool and awaited instructions. The teacher divided them into two teams for a race. A boy from each group would swim a length; when he touched the far end, another boy from his team would dive in; and so on, until one team finished first. Jeffrey's team was holding its own until he jumped in—the only diving he had ever done was from a buffalo's back—and struck out blindly. Twice he bumped into the side and by the time he reached the end of the pool, the opposing side had built up a lead of nearly one length. Looking up at the faces on his own team, Jeffrey saw the first strong emotion he had elicited from a group of people since coming to this school: contempt. Climbing out, he watched his team lose by the length he himself had lost.

Then the teacher ordered everyone back into the pool. He explained that holding the breath increased lung power and enhanced general health. Therefore, he was going to see who in this class could hold his breath the longest. The teacher held up a stopwatch in his brawny hand. "When I count to three, take a breath, go under, and stay under as long as you can."

The boys stood waist deep in the shallow end, while the teacher strolled to the diving board and stood on its tip. During this time Jeffrey took rapid, shallow breaths, sucking in air while thrusting his abdomen out like a quickly worked bellows. Within seconds he felt his lungs filling—as they should by this procedure. When he heard the instructor bark out "one . . . two . . . three!" Jeffrey inhaled with a tremendous rush and went under the water. He closed his eyes and concentrated upon the black screen between his eyebrows, a spot there that he imagined, and slowly but surely—just as the guru had trained him to experience—a small, cloudy space of white light appeared, wavered, pulsed. It was upon this rhythmic light that he focused, letting it absorb his consciousness until, abruptly, he knew his air was gone, and the body summoned him to breathe again. So he rose to the surface and with utmost self-control—for he had been trained for this too—slowly inhaled in one long fluid stroke of his diaphragm.

Gathered around the pool he saw the other boys, all of them staring at him, some with mouths slackly open in wonder. He was alone in the pool.

On the diving board the physical education teacher held the stopwatch, glancing now at it, now at Jeffrey. "Two minutes," he announced in a tone of disbelief, "and twenty-three seconds!"

Jeffrey started to wade to the side.

"Two twenty-three," the teacher repeated incredulously. "Say, what's your name again?"

"Jeffrey Moore, sir."

"Jeffrey Moore, I can't remember anyone beating two minutes in the fifteen years I have been at this school." He stared appraisingly at the slightly built boy. "Okay, free time!" he declared to the class.

For the rest of the period the boys swam, played tag, ducked one another. Jeffrey swam a little, but soon got out and sat against a wall, watching the others—many of whom were now watching him. In the locker room, while dressing, Jeffrey felt a tap on his shoulder. A boy stared curiously at him.

"How did you do that? How did you stay under so long?"

Aside from a few cursory questions, this was the first earnest one put to Jeffrey since he had arrived at the school. So he replied with eagerness: "It's not hard to do once you learn Bhastrika Pranayama."

"Huh?"

"A way of breathing." Jeffrey waved his hand impatiently. "I can show you. My Master taught me. It isn't being so difficult. I can—"

A bell rang; the gym period was finished. The boy turned, hurried back to his locker, and closed it. Boys filed down the line of benches, so Jeffrey finished dressing and left too.

In the hall, walking toward his history class, Jeffrey felt another tap on his shoulder. This time he had to look up and up— It was Tom Carrington, the basketball player.

"Kids are coming over to my house Friday after school. You can come if you want."

Jeffrey nodded. "I thank you," he said, wanting to add, "about that belching I was doing in the cafeteria—I am sorry for it. I did not know better." Instead he said nothing, but watched Tom Carrington stride away. During those final days in the village, when his father had talked so much—wanting to get everything in—they had discussed the feeling of regret. Father had said, "Never regret the past. Save your energy for what is happening right now, at this very moment."

So Jeffrey tried to think of the American Civil War, the subject under discussion in his next class, although in the back of his mind he was savoring his little victory in the swimming pool, as well as hoping his behavior in the cafeteria would soon be forgotten. Robert E. Lee. Ulysses S. Grant. The thing was, he had been noticed today. Vanity, Father would warn. Well, so it was vanity—but it felt good to have held his breath longer than anyone else.

* * *

The rest of the week Jeffrey looked forward to Friday. Back in his village he had never been lonely—at least not until Father died—but with boys his age had played cricket, gone swimming, climbed trees, and with Rama had killed vipers. It seemed that after Father's death, the world had cut him off, isolated him with the powerful memory of a raging fire, a dawn river, and birds rising from the shore. Of course, Aunt Betty had done everything possible to make him comfortable; more than that, she had made him feel that he belonged to the old house. But not until Tom Carrington invited him to his house had Jeffrey felt there was a chance to return to the world as he had known it before Father's death.

On Friday afternoon Jeffrey approached the Carrington house with excitement—and apprehension. When he rang the bell, no one answered for such a long time that he wondered if he had come on the wrong day. Suddenly a woman opened the door and frowned at him. "Go on, they're in the basement—" From her curtness, Jeffrey understood that he should have just gone right in. On the stairway down, he heard the heavy rhythms of rock music blasting from beneath his feet. The light in the basement was dim, except over a billiard table where four boys were playing pool. In a little space beyond the table two couples were dancing. Tom Carrington sat on a couch, drinking a Coke. Next to him was Lucy Smith, a pretty girl with long, braided black hair. Jeffrey had often noticed her in class; Lucy was always ready with an answer when no one else could handle a tough question. Jeffrey walked up to Tom and stood there, not knowing what was expected of him. Both Tom and Lucy eyed him until he just sat down.

"Coke in the fridge," Tom said, waving his hand backward at a bar lined with liquor bottles on glass shelves. Then without another word Tom got up and walked over to study the game of pool.

Maybe, Jeffrey thought, he feels as awkward with me as I do with him—as I do with *all* of them.

"I heard about you," Lucy Smith remarked abruptly. She had braces on her teeth, but was still pretty. "I heard you stayed under water a lot longer than anyone ever did in this school."

Jeffrey was surprised. Aside from one boy in the locker room, nobody had mentioned it.

"They couldn't believe you stayed under so long," continued Lucy, adding, once she looked him up and down, "You sure don't look like someone who could hold his breath two minutes twenty-three seconds. Know what some of the guys did? They asked Hank Foley—he's a big senior tackle on the football team—to hold his breath, and he couldn't get *near* two minutes."

Jeffrey didn't know what a tackle was, but clearly this fellow Hank was strong and far bigger than he was. "Nobody told me about that," he admitted.

The girl laughed. "That's because they can't understand how you did it. How *did* you do it?"

Encouraged by her winsome smile, Jeffrey began to explain the Indian breathing exercises. At her urging he then demonstrated various methods—Bhastrika, Ujjai, Sitali—while music blasted away and new arrivals danced in the corner and some boys racked up the billiard balls for another game of pool. Phil Booker, having lost the last game, ambled over to the couch just as Jeffrey was sticking his tongue out, shaped like a curled leaf, to inhale deeply and demonstate yet another technique.

Hands on hips, Phil asked Lucy, "What in hell is *he* doing?"

She waved him off impatiently and continued to watch Jeffrey suck in air through the tube formed by his protruding tongue.

Phil muttered something under his breath and went away.

Lucy asked what was the reason for doing all these complicated breathing exercises.

"To calm the mind," Jeffrey said.

"Why calm it?"

How could he answer such a question in a basement reverberating with loud music, billiard balls clicking, and people talking and laughing? Even in silence, how could he explain an idea that had been part of his life ever since he could remember? Calming the mind was—well, calming the mind. It was an ideal that everyone in the village acknowledged was essential to happiness, the mark of well-being. So instead of answering such a question, he simply added that there was another dimension to the practice of calming the mind: mantras also helped.

Hands clasped, Lucy leaned forward. "What's a mantra?"

"A chant."

"Magic?"

"No, a prayer."

"You mean, like one of *our* prayers?"

Jeffrey did not want to show his ignorance of Christian prayers, so he replied cautiously, "I would be thinking so."

"Tell me a mantra!" Lucy urged, clapping her hands. "Please! Tell me a mantra!"

Jeffrey hesitated. Why did she want to know? In his experience a mantra was sacred, therefore spoken of solemnly. This girl's carefree eagerness surprised him.

"Please," she wheedled.

A few kids swirled around the couch, one boy asking Lucy to dance, but she waved him away. A girl asked her what was going on. Lucy shook her head impatiently, her eyes fixed on Jeffrey. "Tell me a very, very special mantra," she pleaded.

There was so much noise in the basement that Jeffrey had to lean forward to be heard. "This is the Gayatri—"

Lucy beckoned him. "Sit next to me! Here!"

"No," he said in alarm, "this is okay."

"Please! Otherwise I can't hear you!" She patted the cushion beside her on the couch.

The fact was her invitation stunned Jeffrey. No Indian girl would ask a boy to sit close to her. Yet so compelling was Lucy's smile that he got up and did as she asked.

He edged away slightly when her thigh touched his.

"Now tell me!"

"This is a very sacred mantra, the Gayatri Mantra," he began.

"Wonderful!"

Again her enthusiasm rattled him; yet when she tapped his wrist and repeated, "Tell me!" Jeffrey explained, with mounting enthusiasm of his own, that for Brahman Hindus nothing is more spiritually purifying than the recitation of the Gayatri. He did not add that years ago women were forbidden to hear it.

"Tell me! Say it!"

In a singsong chant—Lucy put her ear close to his mouth to catch the words—Jeffrey began the mantra: "Om tut suh-viter vah ree yen yim—"

"What language is that?" Her face was inches from his.

"Sanskrit."

"That's an Indian language, isn't it."

"Yes, an old one."

"Like Greek and Latin?"

He nodded.

"Tell me more!"

Her ear was disconcertingly close to his mouth, yet Jeffrey chanted through the basement uproar: "Boor-go day-vahs-yah dee moo hee/Dee yo yo nuh pra choo duh yat!"

Lucy gripped his shoulder to pull him even closer. "Say it *again*!"

So Jeffrey chanted, again and again, while Lucy listened with concentration, until she began repeating the syllables under her breath. It occurred to Jeffrey that the girl was memorizing the mantra! He felt proud, as though

97

he had brought something of his own into this basement—a new ability aside from playing billiards or dancing. He had brought something of his past, of his India into this room, and someone had accepted it. He was grateful to Lucy Smith, yet disturbed by her physical closeness and by her eagerness—you didn't learn a mantra the way you put to memory the words of a popular song. For the moment, however, he chanted the mantra into her cupped ear, while the basement vibrated from so much noise.

As he chanted, he could see from the wall clock that it was time to go. Aunt Betty had asked him to be home at seven. That morning she had insisted, for some reason, that he be home on time, maybe because until now he had always gone straight home from school. If only she knew that often for weeks at a stretch he had lived alone in the village, while Father tramped the roads of India!

Lucy was now asking him what the mantra meant in English.

He explained it was a holy prayer to the sun. It meant God beyond God. "Let us all think," he translated, "of the burning light of the Shining Ones so that the divine unmanifest Source may illuminate our minds."

"Say that again?" she asked, grimacing.

"I am sorry, but I must go to home." Jeffrey rose, and, not knowing what else to do, bowed from the waist.

Lucy giggled.

He turned and looked around for Tom Carrington. The tall boy was bent over the billiard table, sighting along a cue stick. Waiting until Tom had taken a shot, Jeffrey went up to him and stood there. Tom looked down at him.

"Thank you," Jeffrey said.

Tom nodded casually and returned to the billiard table. That was all. Jeffrey plodded slowly up the basement stairs, having a last glance at Lucy Smith huddled on the couch, laughing with two other girls.

Once outside in the still air of early evening, he realized how lonely he would have been in Tom Carrington's basement if Lucy Smith hadn't talked to him. Was she really interested in the Gayatri Mantra? Or was she just being nice? At any rate, she had learned after a fashion to chant it. Lucy was quick. After a week's practice, say for a half-hour a day, she would be able to chant the mantra like a Brahman. But why had Tom Carrington even invited him? They had said nothing to each other, and it seemed as if Tom had deliberately ignored him.

The air was crisp, but not cold, not the way it had been for many days. He left his jacket unzipped on the walk home. All the way he kept thinking of those kids in the basement, so filled with energy, so loud, so healthy, so casual and relaxed. It was difficult to know what Americans meant by what they did. In the village they would have been considered impolite, even insolent. In the village, if you were invited to a house, you took care not to disturb the adults. You were quiet and excessively courteous. Upon leaving, you profusely thanked the boy's family—grandmother on down—for rice cakes and tea, bowing your way out of the house. But Tom's mother stayed clear; and he couldn't believe any of those kids would seek her out to pay their respects.

Opening the front door of the old house, Jeffrey was still considering these differences. From the living room came the high, anxious voice of his aunt. "Jeffrey? Is that you? I have been waiting so long! You're late!"

Was he? He couldn't be. Aunt Betty emerged from

the living room and carefully closed the double doors behind her. "Seems like I have been waiting for *hours*!" she exclaimed with a broad smile. "Did you enjoy yourself?" Without waiting for a reply, she added, "Well, don't waste time—go in, go in there!" She thrust him toward the double doors and reopened them herself. "Go on, go *in*!"

When Jeffrey passed the threshold, he noticed, standing in the middle of the room, a bicycle: it had a headlight, hand gear, and chain guard, its shiny chrome flashing in the lamplight.

"That's why I have been waiting so impatiently!" cried Aunt Betty in triumph. "Well? Do you like it? *Do* you?"

Jeffrey ran his fingers along the metal curve of the front fender. It was a beautiful bicycle.

"I just thought," Aunt Betty went on, standing behind him, "you'd need a bike in the spring, so you can ride out of town. Spring is lovely around here."

A beautiful bike. Aunt Betty had no idea how much a bike meant to an Indian: it was a passport to the world. Without one in a village, you were prey to erratic bus schedules and long, tiring walks in the hot sun. A bike was like an arm, a leg, an eye. Jeffrey had never owned one, although Father kept promising that when they "got a little ahead financially," a bike for him would be their first purchase. Of course, they never got a little ahead, they only got farther behind. The scooter that Father used was the property of the Welfare Association; before leaving the village Jeffrey had wheeled the scooter—not risking an accident—to a local official who would store it until the association came for it.

A beautiful bike. He worked the gear and knelt to

inspect the thin, hard tires. A beautiful bike. And yet something was wrong. Not with the bike, but with his having it. Jeffrey glanced up at his beaming aunt. "This is costing very much money."

She waved her hand dismissively. "Nah. Not much."

"But you sold your car, aunt, to save money."

"Because I really didn't need it. Don't worry. Money is no object when a boy needs a bike."

It was like his own father talking. The voice was higher and thinner, but the words were similar: optimistic, care-free—and suspicious. Jeffrey had lived long enough with someone careless of money to recognize the symptoms. His aunt was projecting unfounded assurance, and Jeffrey guessed that she could ill afford to spend so much money. Yet he could not resist the bike, this beautiful bike.

Rising, he went to his aunt, flung his arms around her (he had not done such a thing since his mother was alive), and murmured, "Thank you, thank you, thank you. . . ."

✖   ✖   ✖

Aunt Betty was right: spring was in the air. Riding to school on his new bicycle, he noticed tiny buds on tree limbs, like a string of green beads on a necklace. Where there had been patches of snow a few weeks past, shoots of grass were thrusting out of the brown lawns. He had been in this American town more than a month now. He had a bike, and if not friends, at least kids at school were taking some notice of him. Moreover, he belonged to an old house where his father and aunt had been born in a second-floor bedroom and where old people, his ancestors, regarded him from picture frames across a vast passage of time. Riding his new bike, Jeffrey felt that he might yet call this American town his home and the people in it his friends.

Then something happened that puzzled him and disturbed his new-found equanimity.

In the school hallway, after lunch, he saw two girls halt in the flow of traffic and waggle their heads loosely, like a pendulum—in a south Indian manner. One girl loudly chanted, "Om tut suh-viter vah ree yen yim." The other girl supplied the next line, and both chanted the third in unison. Although kids stopped and gawked at them, they pretended not to notice and went their separate ways.

Twice more that afternoon Jeffrey saw girls stop to chant the Gayatri Mantra, waggling their heads like south Indians. It occurred to him that he must have been waggling his own head every time he said "yes"; the habit of a lifetime is not conscious. They were therefore imitating him. Or more to the point, making fun of him.

Lucy Smith had learned the mantra simply to amuse herself and her friends.

The next day the Gayatri was chanted throughout the halls by both girls and boys. Sometimes they gave him a quick glance of amusement, but more often they ignored him. Maybe, thought Jeffrey, they didn't even know where Lucy had got the words. Whenever he entered a classroom and his eyes met hers, Lucy glanced quickly away. Why had she done this? But then, why not? He and his ways were strange; had Lucy Smith come to live in his village, her nasal American accent, blue jeans, and bangs—and teeth braces—would have seemed odd, perhaps ridiculous to him. Father would have told him to shrug the incident off, and so he would try. After all, what did the mantra mean to him now? Perhaps he no longer believed in mantras or in the gods who had failed to help him when he needed help most. Something wonderful had occurred at the Cauvery River—something too powerful for him to examine yet, something lurking in the far reaches of his mind, like a light hidden behind a door with only a slit of brilliance appearing beneath it—but perhaps that strange experience had nothing to do with mantras, rituals, and prayers to the gods. And yet perhaps in his own village, he would have felt that making fun of a mantra was a terrible sin. Here, on the other hand, he wasn't sure. There were no cows in the street, no scorching noontime heat, no tea stalls, no Irula tribesmen strolling along with reed baskets full of cobras. And there were no temples of Shiva, Hanuman, Krishna. There were Christian temples, but he had not yet been inside one. His aunt had timidly asked one Sunday if he would like to attend church, but on that occasion— new to America and to Christianity—Jeffrey had begged off.

So here he was, walking through the halls of an alien school, while all around him people were mispronouncing the sacred Gayatri Mantra. At least he took comfort in that: not one kid was chanting it properly. According to Hindu practice, the incorrect pronunciation of a mantra simply nullified it. So these kids were reciting a lot of meaningless words. If they expected him to get angry or hurt, he was going to disappoint them. After all, they were mouthing terrible Sanskrit and not even waggling their heads with the fluid motion of a true south Indian!

Only once during the day was he ever directly approached about the mantra. A boy from a grade below him came along and said, "Hey, you're the guy from

103

India, right? What are they doing? I heard they are reciting some voodoo magic from India."

"They are chanting a mantra. Like that."

The boy screwed up his face. "No kidding. What does it mean?"

"It means," Jeffrey said with a grave look, "let us all think of the burning light of the Shining Ones so that the divine unmanifest Source may illuminate our minds."

"Huh?"

"That is the meaning, only you would never be knowing it, would you, from the bad Sanskrit."

The boy's mouth opened slackly. "Yeah? Well, okay. But why are they *doing* it?"

"To be getting the attention of people like you," Jeffrey said.

For a moment the boy stared thoughtfully, then grinned at Jeffrey. "You're right. That's it."

Through the afternoon the mangled Gayatri Mantra drifted above the heads of students passing in the halls. A few glanced curiously at Jeffrey, who smiled back; they looked away.

And then, after school, when Jeffrey was bound for the bike racks, Lucy Smith was just wheeling her own bike out. She couldn't avoid him, although her eyes darted around quickly, seeking an avenue of escape.

Jeffrey stopped in her path.

Her dark, brilliant eyes met his, then Lucy sighed. "Look, I didn't mean any harm. Some of the girls wanted to learn it, just for fun, so I told them."

"You learned it quickly, but you were not teaching the correct pronunciation. The chanting is being done wrong. Shall I show you again?"

Lucy's eyes, level with his, studied him closely. "We

were just having some fun. It's hardly the Lord's Prayer."

"It is a holy Hindu prayer."

"Are you a Hindu?"

Jeffrey couldn't reply to that question. Before his father's death he would have said, "Of course I'm a Hindu." Now he wasn't sure.

Before he said anything, however, the girl added another question, "What did you tell Tom Carrington?"

"Tell him?"

"You must have told him something, because he's sore at us kids."

"I don't understand."

"Tom said the mantra was probably like the Lord's Prayer for an Indian."

"Tom Carrington said like that?" Jeffrey found it hard to believe that the tall, laconic boy had defended him.

"Tom would," Lucy said offhandedly. "Well, *are* you?"

"Am I what?"

"A Hindu."

"I'm not sure," he said frankly.

The girl frowned, as if not believing him. "Which means at least you aren't Christian."

"No. I am not being that."

"Are you sore?"

The use of "sore" was new to Jeffrey, yet in context he understood its meaning. "No, I am not being sore. But I am being surprised."

"At what?"

"That making fun of a prayer would be fun."

The girl's lips trembled. "Don't make so much of it."

"I will not."

"Good!" she snapped and wheeled her bike around him. "We didn't mean anything!"

No, Jeffrey thought, not the way you pronounced the mantra.

That evening he wrote a letter to Rama. He described the transatlantic trip, the feel of cold weather, the look of the old house (as big as your own, Rama!), his nice aunt, the tall kids in his new school. He ended by writing:

I miss you, I miss our swimming and cricket. Do you still bat as well as ever? And have you found anyone to catch vipers with? I'm sure not going to find anyone to catch snakes with me here. But I am not really so lonely. There is my aunt and the house and soon I will know more kids at school. But I miss you. Say hello to Subramanian, Kuppuswamy, and Vasu. Write. Always write.

Your friend,
Ganesh

The Gayatri Mantra vanished from the school corridors within a week. No longer a fad, it was forgotten as quickly as it had been learned. Slowly people began making contact with the boy from India. They borrowed a pencil, asked the time (although Jeffrey didn't own a watch), questioned him about school: Did he like it? Was the work harder where he came from? Were the hours the same? He did like it; here the work was harder for him; the hours were shorter. The questions were polite, but not deeply curious, and never asked with the eagerness he showed in answering them. Yet Jeffrey understood it was only through this slow process that he would fully enter the life of the school. "Patience and hope," his grandfather used to say.

Even so, Jeffrey yearned to bridge the gap between two worlds: one he had not wholly left, the other he had not wholly entered. It occurred to him one warm spring day after school, as he watched some boys running on the cinder track, if perhaps Yoga might answer this need: Yoga, which he had learned in India, but could practice here in America. On the day his father died, Jeffrey had given up Yoga, just as he had given up everything else: the Hindu gods, the village life, his expectations of the future. But watching the boys run, he felt the desire to do his own kind of exercise, to reacquaint himself with something that had meant a lot to him in the past.

Entering the school gym, he found it empty save for Tom Carrington, who was shooting baskets on the court. For a few minutes Jeffrey stood in the entranceway and watched. Tom Carrington rose high in the air and with one big hand, curved at the wrist into a shape reminding Jeffrey of a cobra's hood, held the basketball poised a moment, then drove it down through the net, like a carpenter driving a nail into wood. In his own body Jeffrey felt a sense of exhilaration. He watched the tall boy move with rhythmic grace across the floor, keeping the ball in motion, thumping it up and down with a touch that seemed wonderfully delicate for such huge hands. Abruptly the long body went up into the air, legs together but relaxed as if floating in space, with the arm straight, with the wrist curved like a snake's hood above the basket before the ball struck. Clean. Not even stirring the webbed net.

The sight of this graceful performance gave Jeffrey added encouragement to try Yoga again. Changing into gym shorts in the dressing room, Jeffrey went into the wrestling room laid with mats. Along one wall was a mirror, and for a brief time Jeffrey stared curiously at his image: small, thin, freckle-faced, blond. He recalled that in the village he sometimes went home, lifted the veil from the mirror (no one left a mirror unveiled; it was the custom), and studied his pale skin, his squinting blue eyes, his yellow hair. None of the boys at the Mission School ever looked as rumpled, as uncomfortable as he did. They were made for the sun. How he had envied them their rich brown skin!

Standing on the mat, Jeffrey put the palms of his hands together in a gesture of respect, as if his Yoga master was there to be honored. Then, with determination, Jeffrey began to practice asanas, moving from one pose to another, testing his ability to conform to those patterns that his muscles had learned with such patient effort. With a quickening of his senses, Jeffrey understood nothing had been lost. Here in this American gym his body and mind were recapturing the past. Proceeding from asana to asana—standing, sitting, lying—he understood with deep pleasure that the customs of different countries need not destroy a discipline well learned. He practiced a long time, then showered, dressed, and rode his bike into the darkness, whistling an Indian folk song.

✖   ✖   ✖

"Wait!"

Jeffrey turned and in the street light saw the tall figure of Tom Carrington approaching fast on a bike.

"Wait!" When Tom pulled alongside, he was breathing hard. "You left just as I went into the shower. Thought we could ride together. We go in the same direction."

"I know. I went to your house once."

"Yeah, you did, didn't you," Tom observed sheepishly. "You didn't have much fun."

"Oh, I did!" Jeffrey didn't know what else to say. They rode awhile in silence.

"I'm working these days on my hook shot," Tom said abruptly. "By next season I figure to have it down pretty good."

Jeffrey nodded, without understanding what a hook shot was.

"What I hope for," Tom continued in the earnest tone of someone carrying on a conversation earlier interrupted, "is to be six foot seven or eight, so I can play forward. Forward's my natural position. If I stop growing under six foot six, I'll have to play guard, and I'm not fast enough. If I go past six eight, I'll end up as a center, getting my teeth knocked out under the basket." Pausing, he then added, "So I have about five inches left to grow."

Jeffrey never suspected that Tom Carrington would talk so much.

"I figure on making All State forward as a junior. That's not bragging, that's just confidence. Father says, if you don't have confidence, you don't have anything. Like you, for instance. You have confidence."

"Me?"

"Sure. I peeked in the wrestling room while you were practicing. It's Yoga, isn't it? I saw some on TV."

Jeffrey nodded.

"I never saw it done that good on TV. You did it better. Differently."

The boys pedaled a block before Tom continued, as if having thought out exactly what he wanted to say. "You did Yoga like it was easy. Like you weren't thinking about it. You just did it, like it was part of you."

"That's the way Yoga must be. Thank you," Jeffrey added.

"But I bet it's not easy."

"No, it is not. It is to calm the mind."

Tom cocked his head, puzzled. "Yeah? Don't see how you can be calm while curled up that way, like a pretzel."

Jeffrey said nothing. They rode awhile longer in silence.

"Here's my turn," Tom said and slowed to a halt. "I'll meet you at the bike rack tomorrow night, after we practice. Say, about six? We can ride home together. Okay?"

Jeffrey nodded, so surprised and delighted that he had nothing to say. The two rode off in different directions.

✖   ✖   ✖

And so it began. Each night they met either in the gym or at the bike rack and rode home together. In a half-hour ride they talked about a lot of things—or rather Tom did. Jeffrey had certainly got the wrong impression of him: Tom was open and friendly. He was honest too. He admitted—without embarrassment—that a lot of kids had been shy of Jeffrey. And some called him "The Pale Mouse," because he looked scared.

"But you weren't really scared," Tom observed matter-of-factly. "We stopped calling you 'The Pale Mouse' after you held your breath so long."

"I guess I was a pale mouse," Jeffrey admitted.

"Well, you never said much."

"I was not knowing what to say."

"And when teachers called on you, you jumped to attention!"

"I was taught like that."

"Were you taught to hold your breath so long too?"

"Yes, I can show you."

"I'd like to learn."

It was clear to Jeffrey that everyone, himself as well,

had been foolishly timid. Even Tom confessed one evening, "When I asked you home, I didn't know what to talk about. What do I know about India? It's a big country. People are poor. They have plenty of snakes. Do they really have a lot of cobras?"

Jeffrey explained then not only cobras but banded kraits, Russell's vipers, and sawscale vipers. Each question that Tom asked was an invitation to explain India, and so after a while Jeffrey was talking as much as Tom. He explained the monsoon season: how, where he lived, they had rain only one month a year, and if they didn't receive enough water to last the other eleven months, there was drought, famine, and death. He described getting up at dawn to bathe in the river alongside buffaloes. For breakfast he'd have strong coffee with hot milk and rice cakes eaten with a coconut chutney. He told of rice-planting time, when women in bright saris would wade through the flooded paddies, transplanting the tender shoots while their employer stood on the bank under a black umbrella. With other boys he played cricket outside the village; his friend Rama, even smaller than he was, was a great batsman who wanted someday to play with the All India team against Pakistan. There was a lot of sickness in the village. People died of typhoid, dysentery, and malaria. There were lepers too with only knobs for fingers and stumps for feet. At night you could see all of the stars above the palm trees, because only a couple of houses were as tall as three stories.

Tom would listen and mutter, "Yeah." Gravely, he took in these impressions of another world.

Soon they were walking together down the halls of school. Because of his association with the basketball player, Jeffrey was quickly accepted by other boys, especially athletes. A few times Tom even brought them to watch Jeffrey do asanas in the wrestling room. In silence they stood around while he slipped easily from one pose to another, twisting, gliding through an internal silence into "pretzels," as Tom called asanas. A few boys tried—Phil Booker, an all-around athlete, tried especially hard—but none could do the Supta Kurmasana, the tortoise pose, or Urdhva Kukkutasana, the strutting cock, both of which required not only strength but uncommon suppleness and balance. Finally, with a scowl and a curse of defeat, Phil Booker gave up. A football player, staring appraisingly at Jeffrey, said, "Maybe you're small, but you're some athlete." Jeffrey volunteered to teach them asanas. "If I can do them, you sure can," he acknowledged generously.

Afterward, biking home with Tom, he asked why those fellows took him for an athlete.

"To do that stuff you *have* to be an athlete," Tom observed sensibly.

Jeffrey accepted the explanation, but could not really think of himself as athletic. In the village the practice of asanas was merely a prelude to meditation. Jeffrey's guru would have laughed contemptuously at the idea of Yogis being athletes. He would have dropped Jeffrey as a student had the boy thought of these physical exercises as being anything more than preparation for spiritual ones.

But the fact that Tom and the other boys accepted him was enough for Jeffrey. Moreover, his skill at Yoga, voiced through the halls, enhanced his reputation with girls as well, all save Lucy Smith, who had stayed clear of him ever since their meeting at the bike rack and their talk about the Gayatri Mantra. Now and then, during class, Jeffrey would feel someone looking at him from behind and turn his head quickly in Lucy's direction. Sometimes he caught her eye, but she never gave him time to smile.

It was nearly the end of the spring semester. With sunlight remaining longer, he and Tom rode out of town into the countryside, a green checkerboard of newly planted corn and wheat fields, with red silos glittering in the blue air. Or they biked to a high bluff overlooking the Mississippi River. Panoramic miles of midwestern farmland receded until at the horizon they merged in color with the sky. Jeffrey liked this view. It reminded him of the vastness of India—the raw power, the awesome beauty of it. "What is that?" he once asked, pointing across the river, near the bridge, where a lot of tractors, graders, and other machines were parked.

"The new highway," said Tom. "Once across the bridge and through town, that highway is going to head for the state capital."

To Jeffrey it had the appearance of a long, flat snake at this distance, with a white stripe down its back, crawling through the green land.

"Do you have highways like it in India?" Tom asked.

Jeffrey laughed. "In our village we have two narrow paved roads. The rest are being dirt."

One evening when Tom veered off to follow his own street home, he halted abruptly and said, "Have you got a nickname? Jeffrey is really stiff."

"In the village they called me Ganesh."

"Ganesh? What kind of name is that?"

"The name of an elephant-headed god."

Tom chuckled. "You let people call you *that*?"

Jeffrey waggled his head, south Indian fashion. "Ganesh is the Remover of Obstacles. Yes, I liked it."

"If you liked it there, you might as well be called the same thing here. From now on, you're Ganesh." Tom waved and rode off into the darkness.

After dinner that night, while Aunt Betty watched television, Ganesh wrote another letter to Rama, describing the tall athlete who had befriended him, his daily life at school, his wonderful new bike. He had nearly finished the letter when it occurred to him that he had asked nothing about the village, nothing about his friend.

So after a long thoughtful pause he wrote:

I must never forget you and our friendship. It is easier for me to forget than it is for you. Do you see? I am living in a new world, but you remain in the one we shared. So you must tell me everything. You must keep my memory alive. I count on you, my friend.

Yours,
Ganesh

Part 3

In the last weeks of the spring semester Ganesh moved deeper into his new life. When a teacher asked him to give the class a talk on India, he accepted—encouraged by Tom Carrington, who bluntly pointed out that "anybody who can turn into a pretzel can talk to a bunch of kids." So Ganesh told them the same things he had privately told Tom. Then other teachers invited him to talk. He accepted their invitations too, emboldened by success. Each time he spoke there was a change in him physically. The first time he stood stiffly, hands flat against his sides in the Mission School style of recitation. The second time his hands began to relax, the fingers even curled a little, and one leg took his weight. The third time he smiled and finally looked straight into the eyes of his audience. He had not yet mastered the American accent, much less idiom, and whenever he confused *v*'s and *w*'s, the kids giggled, but Ganesh didn't mind at all. What mattered was their calling him "Ganesh" in the hallways between classes.

The last week of school was approaching, and Ganesh had a goal in mind: he wanted to ask some of the kids to his house. The problem was, he didn't know what to do with them once they came. He lacked both a phonograph and a knowledge of American music, let alone the ability to dance to it; unlike Tom, he didn't have a pool table to provide entertainment. Back in the village, kids often went for a walk or sat under a tree watching the sunset. It was enough there. But Ganesh realized that here the kids wanted more to do. He decided therefore to begin modestly by having only one person home—his friend Tom—before asking others.

One evening as they rode together, he asked Tom shyly, "Will you come to my house for tea tomorrow?"

"For *what*?"

"For tea and biscuits."

After a long pause, Tom agreed. When they parted, he observed with a wry smile, "It's the first time I was ever invited for *tea*."

Ganesh was pleased, excited, and shaken by the acceptance. He pestered Aunt Betty with instructions about tea the next day. She must get tasty biscuits—he meant cakes—and Darjeeling tea and some other sweets. She laughed. There was only one gourmet shop in town and if this Darjeeling tea wasn't there, it was nowhere to be found.

Ganesh was not deterred. At least the tea must be prepared from *loose leaves*; the American tea bag would not provide a proper taste.

"Yes, your highness," his aunt gave him a low bow.

116

The next day, when the two boys biked up to the house, it was sunset; the tall gray house loomed high above the tree tops, now ringed with a liquid orange light.

Getting off his bike, Tom stared up at the weather vane. "I've seen this house before. When I was a little kid, I thought it was haunted. So did other kids."

Ganesh was puzzled. "Why?"

"Because it's so old."

When they entered the house, Aunt Betty was waiting in the parlor. Ganesh noticed at once there was something different about her. Usually she greeted him with a cheery hello, some chatter. Today she was oddly subdued and hardly spoke to Tom. Her face seemed drawn, her eyes large and sad. This sudden change from her usual buoyancy startled Ganesh, who watched curiously as she brought in the tea tray and then silently left the room. It rattled Ganesh, who was already nervous about hosting the tea.

Tom seemed ill at ease too, as he stared at the tea pot. When Ganesh poured tea into two little cups, the big basketball player unsteadily lifted his with both hands. The cup seemed lost in them. Suddenly Ganesh realized that Tom had probably never drunk from such a fragile cup in his life. Back in the village the kids drank milky tea from water glasses; it was a mark of status there to have the chance to drink from real tea cups. At any rate, his friends in the village drank tea, had consumed it from infancy. Tom, however, took a small hesitant sip, grimaced, and carefully set the cup down. Fortunately Aunt Betty had made brownies for the occasion. Relieved of the tea cup, Tom proceeded to devour three or four of them rapidly.

Perhaps the formality of tea created an awkwardness between the boys; silence grew in the waning light.

"My great-grandfather," Ganesh remarked suddenly and pointed to the portrait above the fireplace.

"He looks pretty tough," commented Tom.

"He was strong," Ganesh said proudly. "He built this house with his own two hands."

Tom whistled in polite admiration.

Another silence followed, after which, for want of something else to do, Ganesh suggested that they go up to his room.

"This is a big house," Tom said on the stairway. "Your great-grandfather really built the whole thing?"

"When he was not advocating."

"Advocating?"

"Practicing the law," Ganesh explained.

In the room Tom sat self-consciously at the desk, his long legs angled out awkwardly as if unable to find enough space.

Ganesh felt a touch of panic. Maybe this invitation had been a mistake. Back in the village, if he and a friend got bored, they could always have a race rolling bicycle tires down a path or see who could catch the largest bullfrog in a nearby pond (once he had caught one measuring almost two feet). But here he was with his American friend, sitting in silence in a room that didn't contain a stereo, a single game, a hobby craft project, or anything else geared to an American imagination.

So, fumbling in a side drawer of the desk, Ganesh came out with a dog-eared snapshot taken of his parents many years ago, when he had not yet been born. It was the only photo of them he had.

Father wore a plain loincloth and three ash marks of

the Shivaite sect of Hinduism across his forehead. Mother, small and frail, was enveloped in a flowing sari, a red dot in the middle of her forehead.

Ganesh handed the frayed photo carefully to his friend. "My parents."

Wrinkling his brow, biting his lip nervously, Tom stared at the photo a long time. "Your parents?"

"Yes. Like that."

"I thought they were American."

"Yes, born in this country. My father here in this town. My mother in Ann Arbor city in the state of Michigan."

"But—" Tom tapped the photo, quizzically. "They are dressed like Indians, aren't they?"

"They lived like Indians. Mother used to say, 'Scratch our white skin and you'll find the dark skin of India.' See those lines on my father's forehead? They are meaning he was a devotee of Lord Shiva."

"Who's Lord Shiva?"

For a moment Ganesh was shocked. How could anyone, even an American, not know of Lord Shiva? "A god of the Hindus," he explained.

Tom handed the photo back. "Do you believe in Shiva too?"

"I don't know," Ganesh said simply. "I did once, but I am not knowing now."

"They're dead, aren't they."

"Yes. I came here because my father died."

"We heard that," Tom said gently. He slapped his knee. "Well, are you getting used to us?"

"I am, yes, I am. Thank you." Ganesh glanced around the room at the old bed, the figured wallpaper, the window overlooking the yard. "Yes, I am feeling now part of this house."

Tom laughed. "How can you feel part of a *house*?"

"I do."

There was another awkward silence, during which Tom placed two huge hands on two knobby knees. He looked around restlessly, his mouth working to find words for a conversation. At last he said, "Do you miss India?"

"Of course."

"Would you like to be back there?"

"I don't know," Ganesh said honestly. "I am now being part of two places."

Tom beat a faint tattoo on his knees with the palms of his hands; he was trying—it was obvious to Ganesh—but failing to hide his boredom.

So Ganesh took a breath and said boldly, "I am asking for a favor, Tom."

"Sure. What is it?"

"Teach me how to make friends happy when they are coming to my house."

Tom screwed up his face. "Hey, there's nothing you should do! Let 'em take care of themselves."

"Because I can't dance, I don't know your games, or what you talk about or your sports, do I?"

Staring hard at him a moment, Tom sighed. "Yeah, I see what you mean. But you shouldn't worry, you'll get on to everything. The guys like you."

"Do they actually?"

"Sure they do. Girls too. See, you don't cause trouble. And you listen to what people say. So don't worry." Tom got up, his big hands smoothing back his hair nervously. "I got to be going."

Downstairs, at the front door, Tom turned and said with a smile, "So don't worry."

"Yes, it's what my father would say too." Ganesh stood

in the doorway watching until his friend's bike vanished in the gathering dusk. It was not always easy to take good advice. "Don't worry." Very good advice, only he still didn't dance or know American games or what the kids talked about or how to play their sports. Then he went inside and searched for his aunt, who was not downstairs. He went up to her bedroom and knocked. At first he thought she was not there, but then he heard rustling; he was not sure Aunt Betty would come to the door, until slowly it swung open.

His aunt's eyes were red and swollen. She gripped a Kleenex as she let him into the room. "Has your friend gone? Seems like a nice boy. So tall, though. Did you like the brownies? That was Darjeeling tea you had." Aunt Betty talked as she shuffled toward the bed and wearily eased down on its edge.

Ganesh stood near the door. In the light of a bedside lamp his aunt's face seemed older than before. The light made dark hollows under her cheekbones and emphasized the lines across her forehead, the steel gray amidst her light brown hair. Aunt Betty dabbed at her eyes with the Kleenex, then wadded and unwadded it with both hands. "Yes," she said as if answering a question, "it happens that way. You're fine when there's two of you, but alone you're prey to anything coming along. Sit down, Jeffrey."

He sat next to the window, lit now by a slant of street light. A maple branch tapped against the pane, a hectic motion that added to the tension he felt in the presence of his aunt, who continued to talk—not only to him but to herself as well.

"Never did tell you about your Uncle Henry. People said a lawyer's daughter shouldn't marry a garage mechanic, but I paid no attention. And how right I was! We had twenty-eight good years together, and I never regretted one moment I spent with Henry Strepski. That box of Kleenex, please." She pointed toward the dresser. "I am so upset, boy, so upset. What was I saying?"

Ganesh handed her the box of Kleenex. "You were saying about Uncle Henry."

"Yes, my Henry. We never had children. Couldn't. And people say that makes a couple closer. Well, I don't know, but I do know we were close. And Henry proved himself to everyone. He started as a mechanic, but when he went to the state capital to file papers for a new garage, he already owned *three*." Her bemused tone lifted suddenly. "Henry was like your father, Jeffrey. Couldn't keep a red cent in his pocket. If someone asked him for a loan, Henry would just wave his hand and say, 'Sure, don't worry, how much?' in a whisper so other people wouldn't know. When he died, I had no idea how many debts were owed him. Of course, some people came forward and paid, but many did not. Jeffrey?"

"Yes, ma'am?"

She ran her hand through the frizzled hair. "He was killed in a car accident that day on the way to the state capital to file those papers for the new garage. That old road has terrible curves. A truck came around one of them blind—" There was a long silence.

"I am sorry," Ganesh said quietly. He added, "I know how you are feeling."

Wiping her eyes, Aunt Betty said, "Yes, I suppose you do." She appraised him closely. "I suppose you do. Come here."

Ganesh went to the bed. She held out her hand and he took it. "Five years now, Jeffrey, and I have missed him every day. Sometimes I think I hear him downstairs, coming home from work." She smiled wanly and let go of Ganesh's hand. "Isn't that crazy?"

"No," said Ganesh.

"Five years. And he has never left my thoughts," Aunt Betty continued, not having heard her nephew. "Sometimes I feel he is here in this house."

"He is," Ganesh affirmed. "He is everywhere. So are my parents."

But Aunt Betty, still in her bemused state of mind, did not hear him. "Now that Henry's gone, I am easy prey. I always heard people say it, now I know it's true: a widow hasn't a chance."

"I am not understanding."

She glanced up at her nephew, who stood near the bed. "Why, now that I haven't a husband to defend my rights, the state has decided to take this house. Boy, we are going to lose it."

×   ×   ×

The next day for Ganesh went by in a waking dream. There were semester examinations, but he could scarcely remember them. "We are going to lose the house": those words throbbed in his mind like wounds, while he tried to think past them into the answers for history and science.

That evening, after classes, he went to the gym, knowing he would find Tom there shooting baskets. They had hardly spoken during the day.

And there Tom was, running in a leisurely way up and down the court, feinting and eluding imaginary opponents, then abruptly tensing his tall, thin body for a drive at the basket. When he saw Ganesh standing in the gym doorway, Tom waved. He took aim and let go of the ball; it whooshed through the net. "That was a set shot by Jerry West!" Then he tried other shots: a dunk like Bill Walton, a drive and twisting layup like Julius Erving—singing out the names of professional stars when he made the basket, keeping silent when he missed. At last, dripping sweat, he tucked the ball under one arm and walked over to Ganesh.

"Can you believe the exams are over?" he exclaimed with a smile. "How did you do?"

"I don't know."

Tom laughed. "Sounds like you don't care."

"No, I am not caring."

"Well, come on, you got to care a *little*," Tom replied, staring curiously at his friend. "Is anything wrong?"

So Ganesh told him: the state government wanted the old house for its new highway. He tried to recall words and phrases used by his aunt. After two years of proceedings, the court had finally decided in favor of the state. There were no more avenues of appeal, no stays of executing the order for dispossession. In one week the state would have the right to pull the house down and bring in the road.

Tom let the basketball drop from his hand; it bounced across the court and came to rest against a wall.

"That's some bad luck," Tom said. "*Damn* them! Where are you going to live?"

"There."

"Where?"

"In our house."

Tom scratched his head. "But you just said the state's going to take it over."

"I won't leave."

124

"Look, Ganesh, you got to."

"I won't leave."

"Yeah? How are you going to swing *that*?"

"I don't know." Ganesh turned to go. "But I will be telling you tomorrow."

Tom put his hands on his hips. "Are you serious? You got to be kidding."

Ganesh kept walking.

"Hey! Are you serious?"

Ganesh said over his shoulder, "Yes, I am."

Tom watched his small friend striding out of the gym. On impulse the tall basketball player shouted, "If you need any help, let me know!"

x   x   x

That evening after dinner Ganesh went to his room and dug into the bottom drawer of the dresser where, under some shirts, he had stuffed the bronze idol of Ganesh, his namesake god. Not once, until now, had he taken the idol out, even to look at it. Because it represented something he might not believe in any longer. The truth was, he didn't know. In the village he had often prayed in Hindu fashion to the little figure of the elephant-headed god. He had done "puja": made offerings of sandalwood paste, flowers, coconuts, bananas, and incense to it, reciting a mantra in its praise. Om Shri Maha Ganapataye Namah—Salutations to Ganapati the Great. Before his father had sickened and died, Ganesh used to derive satisfaction from his prayers and rituals, as they seemed to bring him close to a power beyond himself, to link him with it somehow. But betrayed by the gods, he had never again done puja. "Save my father," he had begged, but they had turned a deaf ear or had vanished.

Would he ever again do puja? Ganesh sat the idol on his desk; in the village he would have placed an offering of mimosa petals at the fat deity's feet. Now he simply looked at the belly, the four arms, the elephant trunk and ears, the small eyes, the tall ornate crown on its broad head. What should he do with it? He would not supplicate the god for help, that was one thing; and yet staring at it returned him in memory to the dim interiors of Hindu temples, filled with fire and camphor smoke; with the sweet fragrance of sandalwood.

Abruptly he closed his eyes and brought his palms together in the attitude of prayer before Great Ganapati. He did not ask for anything, yet with eyes closed and hands held together in the submissive pose of puja, he felt a calm descend upon him. For a long while he remained in this position, then opened his eyes and felt stronger. Did he *really* feel stronger? He did. Was it because of the little bronze Ganesh? He did not know. But he knew this: he would not leave this house. It was exactly as he had told Tom Carrington; he and his aunt would not leave when the authorities tried to claim the property. They would sit and not move. Because this was their home, they belonged here, and nothing, not even a government, not even that of the United States of America, was going to remove them.

This is what he would tell Tom Carrington tomorrow: we are going to practice Satyagraha.

The idol of Ganapati, the elephant-headed Ganesh, remained on the desk.

✖   ✖   ✖

Arriving at school early the next day, Ganesh waited at the bike rack for Tom. When the tall boy came along,

Ganesh said immediately, "I have decided to practice Satyagraha."

Looking down with a smile, Tom said, "Meaning what?"

"I mean to be sitting on the porch. I will persuade the government they have been making a mistake."

Tom shrugged in resignation. "Look here, Ganesh, the cops will just carry you out and bring the bulldozers in."

"Then I will come back," Ganesh declared. "Until the government is seeing its error and puts the highway somewhere else."

Tom grimaced. "I can't believe you mean it."

"I do."

"What does your aunt say?"

"I have not yet told her."

Tom lifted his hamlike hands in a gesture of exasperation. "How can you convince anybody of anything by sitting on a porch? No one is going to listen."

"They will have to listen. That is the way of Satyagraha. It is meaning 'a grip on the truth.' I have the truth— we must live in the house of Great-grandfather. Why? Because he built it with his two hands for us. When the government is knowing the same, then the house will be saved."

Tom slowly shook his head. "Damn if you aren't serious. I keep thinking you can't be. And then I know you are." Tom started walking toward the school entrance into which dozens of students were funneling. "Well, count me in," he said with resigned sigh. "I'll sit too."

"I thank you."

"Misery loves company. So maybe we can get some other kids in on it too. When do you need them?"

Ganesh explained that the government took legal possession next Tuesday.

"School's out then. That's good, because kids will be looking for something to do, if they don't have summer jobs—and jobs are scarce this summer. Maybe a few will come over." There was a new-found note of enthusiasm in Tom's voice. "It's like a sit-in. They used to have them at the university. These college kids took over the president's office, sang songs, smoked pot, and got thrown in jail. They had a lot of fun. But they were college kids and could do it."

"I am not meaning like that."

Tom regarded his small friend closely. "I don't know what you mean. But let's get some kids together and let you explain it to them. We'll ask them over to your place on Monday." He added with a smile, "Here's your chance to entertain friends."

So at lunch time, between classes, and after school for the next two days, both boys went about enlisting volunteers. Some kids laughed. Others were indifferent. But more than a dozen—intrigued by the idea of challenging the entire state government—promised to show up at the old house on Monday afternoon.

On the last day of school, Ganesh was walking toward the bike rack when he saw Lucy Smith. This time she was standing in *his* path. Her pretty face was solemn, her lips determinedly thin, her eyes brilliant and judgmental. "I heard about your house," she began. "I'm sorry."

"I thank you."

"You and Tom have asked a lot of kids to help, but you didn't ask me."

Ganesh didn't know what to say, but felt uncomfortable under the steady gaze of this blunt-speaking pretty girl. "You still hold the Gayatri Mantra against me," she observed.

"No, but we are not friends."

His candor surprised Lucy, but only for a moment. Cocking her head in frank appraisal of him, she said with a smile, "It really doesn't matter if we are friends or not. You need people to help you, although nobody seems to know what you've got up your sleeve. The thing is, I don't have a job, so I can spare the time. So I'll be there next Monday." She brushed past him without another word and continued on her way.

✕ ✕ ✕

Ganesh's next problem was to convince his aunt that they must fight for the old house. He now knew her well enough to admire her deep feelings, but to suspect her resolve. After dinner, when they were sitting quietly in the parlor, Ganesh studied her awhile. It seemed that she had become listless, oddly silent. Taking a breath of resolution, he began to explain in a soft, measured voice exactly what sort of idea he had in mind to save the house. She listened as if riveted to the chair, her eyes becoming rounder and larger the longer he spoke. At last she shook her head sadly. "Boy, you know we can't do a thing like that."

"We will, ma'am."

The woman sighed wearily. "I have tried every avenue of the law, but none works." She explained that the state had proved its case for confiscating the land in the public interest; nothing could change it except the commissioner of highways—and that with great effort. All other such lawsuits had been settled; all the stores and residences in the path of the highway construction had been evacuated, and all the evicted people had been duly compensated according to law.

"Now we are the last ones," she concluded.

"Can the road be going somewhere else?"

"That was the question my lawyer asked. Why not take the hamburger drive-in instead—it's two lots to the west."

"Yes, why not? Like that."

"Because, Jeffrey, the drive-in is owned by a big food chain with political connections. It doesn't do much business, but the food chain wants to hold onto the land. Maybe to build on it later."

"We must be persuading the government to put their road through the drive-in."

Aunt Betty gave him a grimace and a smile. "Do you have any idea what I mean?"

"You mean the government is not knowing how much we need this house."

"That is not at all what I mean. First, it is a fact of life that you can't fight money and power. Second, we simply can't defy the law and get away with it."

Ganesh sat ramrod straight in the chair. No one was going to dissuade him from his course of action. He would even stand against his aunt. "A hamburger place is not a home," he declared simply. From where he sat, Ganesh could see the old man staring down from the mantelpiece in a black suit. "Great-grandfather," he said in a slow, emphatic voice, "would be wanting us to save the house he built."

Aunt Betty did not reply immediately, but sat in thought, looking old, tired, and small.

Ganesh did not move, awaiting her response.

At last Aunt Betty thumped the arm of her chair hard. "Jeffrey, I see your great-grandfather in you—his determination. It wasn't there so powerfully in either your grandfather or your father. It has come down whole to you."

Ganesh still did not move, but sat there erect, determined. "We must be ready on Tuesday for the police when they come."

The woman sighed, then clapped her hands down on her knees in a decisive gesture. "You win, boy. We'll be ready."

✳   ✳   ✳

From the top step of the porch, where he sat alongside Tom Carrington, he saw them straggling into the yard, squinting curiously at the weather vane turning in a summer breeze. He watched the kids stroll casually up the cement walk, past the privet bushes and small tulip bed that Aunt Betty hadn't been able to coax into full bloom this year. They stared at the peeling clapboard of the old house, at the old-fashioned wooden scrollwork above the heavily curtained windows. To them, he realized, it was a strange, maybe even a forbidding place, an outcast among the houses of this town even as he himself was an alien among his schoolmates. How could they know that the polished banisters, the faintly creaking floorboards, the slant of light against darkly paneled walls, all whispered to him of a distant past that had come forward into his life? For a moment, seeing them all new, bold, and American, his resolve wavered. They said hello casually or merely waved and sat down in the grass in a semicircle in front of the porch, observing him critically, waiting for an explanation.

"Go on," urged Tom from the side of his mouth. "Tell them!"

These words of crisp command, uttered by a friend, had the effect on Ganesh of unleashing a torrent of words. He had never spoken so quickly, so earnestly. He told them that tomorrow the police would take the house, but only because the government never understood how much it meant to the people who lived here. Once this fact was understood by the authorities, they would move the road elsewhere. It was that simple. Of course, they must first be convinced of the truth, and a firm grip on the truth was the heart of Satyagraha. His father had explained it to him. It was a way of showing your opponents, if they were wrong, that in fact they *were* wrong. To practice Satyagraha, you first had to control a vital piece of territory. In this case, obviously it was the house. You sat in it, refusing to leave no matter what happened. At this point the authorities, no doubt puzzled, would try to figure out why you behaved so stubbornly, at the risk of some kind of punishment. What was so important about an old house? Why did people sit on its porch and refuse to leave? Maybe then the authorities would think about their decision to tear down the house—think about it in a new way, beyond mere rules and regulations, into the lives of the people who cared so much for it.

"They'll kick you out," someone yelled impatiently.

Ganesh shook his head. "We will come back. We must be gaining their respect by being serious."

"Ah, you're just talking about a sit-in," someone else said.

Ganesh shook his head again. "It will become more than just sitting. You will see."

"In what way more than just sitting?"

"That will be depending on our opponents," said Ganesh.

"What if our parents come and drag us away?" a boy asked.

"Come back."

"Yeah? Easier said than done."

"Come back."

"Do we stay overnight?"

"Every night."

"For how long?"

"Until the government tells us the house stays."

"That won't happen," a girl muttered.

"How can they change their mind now?" Lucy Smith asked. "Isn't the road already planned through here?"

"The road can be moved to the left," Ganesh explained.

Lucy persisted. "How do you know that?"

"Because so far the road to this house is only on a map, isn't it?"

A kid got up, brushed the seat of his jeans, and said briskly, "I don't want any part of this nutty thing." He turned and walked away.

"I got a question," said another. "What reason do we give our parents for breaking the law?"

There was a deep silence, through which the light summer breeze whistled idly, like a random thought. Everyone, Ganesh included, understood that this was the essential question. Without an answer to it, none of them would return tomorrow.

Tom Carrington leaned forward and said, before Ganesh could reply to the question, "Tell your parents you have got to help a friend who needs help because he's being treated unfairly. Tell them that and don't back down."

There was another long silence. Then someone called out, "Yeah, but help him do *what*? Stay in an old house like this?"

"It means a lot to him," Tom argued. Then he added, almost as if realizing the truth for the first time, "It sort of means everything to him."

"Yeah? Why?"

This time it was Ganesh who answered. "Because I belong to this house. Because it is the only thing I have been belonging to in my life." He paused. "And because it is all my aunt has left."

"Any more questions?" Tom asked. He got to his feet. "If not, then we'll see you here tomorrow morning bright and early."

Silently the kids rose too and left the yard, either singly or in small groups.

"Will they come back tomorrow?" Ganesh asked Tom, when they were all gone.

The basketball player shrugged. "Who knows."

✗   ✗   ✗

And the next morning they did come—or at least ten of fourteen did. They came with overnight bags, silently trooping up the cement walk, and deposited their gear in upstairs rooms assigned to them by Aunt Betty. She seemed overwhelmed by their presence, and kept muttering, "They're here; they really are *here*." Throughout the morning she appeared with trays of cookies, potato chips, and Cokes, while the Satyagrahis—Ganesh called them this—lolled on the grass, on the porch, playing card games or checkers.

Lucy Smith threw a checkerboard at Ganesh's feet. "Do you play?" she asked. When he nodded, the girl sat down and took the checkers from a box. They played a game; she won. They played another game; she won. They were starting the third game, when someone called out, "Here comes trouble!"

A squad car was pulling up in front of the peeling white fence.

"Go tell my aunt, please," Ganesh said. Lucy nodded and went into the house, while the other Satyagrahis left the yard and congregated on the porch.

Ganesh sat alone on the top step.

"It's Chief of Police Halstead," someone whispered behind him.

The man coming up the walk was very tall. He wore blue pants, black boots, a billed cap, but no gun belt. Approaching within ten or twelve feet of the porch, as if reaching an invisible wall, the police officer pushed his cap back from his forehead and said to the group on the porch, "Where is Mrs. Strepski?"

"She will be coming, sir," Ganesh told him.

The police officer, waiting in silence, gave the kids a puzzled glance, then turned his gaze to the scraggly tulip bed, the oak and maple trees dotting the yard. There weren't many houses left in town with so many old trees.

When Aunt Betty appeared in the doorway, the police officer touched the bill of his cap. "Good morning, Mrs. Strepski," he said.

"Good morning, officer." Aunt Betty sat on the porch swing, its rusty hinges creaking at the motion.

"Hot already and not even noon."

"It does look like an early June scorcher," she offered politely.

"That's my guess too. Mrs. Strepski, I suppose you know why I am here."

"Yes, officer, I do."

"Time's up at noon today. Then you must vacate." He squinted in the glare at the line of kids on the porch, standing like spectators at a game. "Are you packed and ready to leave?"

"No, officer," Aunt Betty replied in a thin voice.

He squinted at her. "Then I can give you until tomorrow morning."

"I appreciate it, officer, only—" She stopped, unable to pronounce the words of defiance. "Only—"

Ganesh spoke up. "We are not leaving the house, sir."

The police chief swiveled his head slowly and looked curiously at the blond freckle-faced boy sitting on the top porch step. "What did you say, fella?"

"We are not leaving the house, your honor."

Screwing his face up in consternation, the policeman turned to the woman in the swing. "Who is this kid?"

"My nephew. Jeffrey Moore."

"Jeffrey Moore, perhaps you can give this to your aunt." He pulled a sheet of paper from his back pocket, gained the porch steps in a few rapid strides, and thrust the paper into Ganesh's hand. "It's the order for eviction." Turning, he walked back to his original spot on the cement walk.

Ganesh handed the paper back—it went from hand to hand until reaching Aunt Betty.

"I will give you until tomorrow morning, Mrs. Strepski," declared Chief Halstead.

"No, your honor," said Ganesh. "We will not be leaving."

The police chief turned to the woman in the swing, who was holding the eviction order in both hands as if ready to wring it like a wet towel. "Does your nephew speak for you?"

She nodded, wordlessly.

"The law says this is now state property," the policeman said crisply to Ganesh. "I don't think you fully understand."

Ganesh said, "The law can move its road so we can stay in our house."

The police chief blinked rapidly. He pushed the cap farther back on his head, until it threatened to slip off. "I am authorized to remove the occupants," he was staring at the whole crew of kids on the porch, "and their possessions from this house at my discretion. Does everyone understand what I am saying?"

Ganesh, seeming to ignore this declaration, replied, "My great-grandfather built this house with his two hands." He was sitting in the full lotus position of Yogis: left foot on right thigh, right foot on left thigh. He felt immovable, like a rock, his spine traveling straight down through his body into the floorboards of the porch and farther down into the earth itself, anchoring there in hot granite.

The policeman did not have a reply for Ganesh's claim that his ancestor had built this large, rambling, half-decayed house with his two hands. He mumbled, "Yes, well, I'm sorry." He stared with disapproval at the other kids on the porch. "What are you all doing here anyway?"

"They are staying with us in the house," Ganesh explained.

"Then they can be removed too."

"They will all come back."

The police chief smiled bitterly. "Not if their parents say no."

"Then," Ganesh said, drawing in a deep breath, "they will not eat!"

"What?"

"They will not eat until they are being allowed to come back here."

Police Chief Halstead took off his cap and wiped his brow. Replacing the cap, he turned and strode to the squad car, which took off with an angry screeching of tires.

When the car had disappeared, the porch filled with voices and sighs of relief and giggling.

"I don't think the chief is used to being bucked that way," someone said.

"Hey, Ganesh, you don't call a cop 'your honor'!"

A boy walked up to Ganesh and glared hard at him. "Who told you to say we wouldn't eat?"

Ganesh shrugged. "I was taking a chance. Like that." He caught the eye of Lucy Smith, who smiled back approvingly.

But in the swing Aunt Betty sat fanning her sweaty face with the eviction order. In a soft, musing tone she asked the summer air, "What's going to happen now?"

* * *

That afternoon a well-dressed woman entered the yard, closed the gate behind herself carefully, and walked toward some of the Satyagrahis who were lolling on the grass near the front porch. Sitting on the top step, Ganesh watched.

"Is Mrs. Strepski here?" the woman asked, lightly scratching a rouged cheek with a manicured nail. "And my daughter? Ruth Hoving?"

A girl got up silently and went into the house. Soon

Aunt Betty came onto the porch, looked at the woman, and frowned.

"Do you remember me, Mrs. Strepski? I'm Dorothy Hoving."

"Yes, I remember you," Aunt Betty said coldly. "My husband had business with yours."

The woman glanced at her shoes, as if embarrassed. "Your husband was a fine man, Mrs. Strepski."

Aunt Betty stood there in stony silence, waiting for the woman to continue. Ganesh figured that whatever business the two men had had between them did not end well. Maybe Mrs. Hoving's husband had borrowed money. Mrs. Hoving bit her lip and glanced nervously at the woman on the porch. Sunlight fell into Mrs. Hoving's eyes, making her squint, and beads of sweat appeared on her make-up, but Aunt Betty did not invite her into the shade.

"I know how you feel," Mrs. Hoving said impulsively. "Losing the house this way. But you must understand my position too. I mean, Ruth—that's my daughter, Ruth—she's so young. I can't let her stay in this house with all these boys." She glanced around, shading her eyes to look at the Satyagrahis, most of them ranged on the porch. "It's a crying shame the state is taking your place. My husband says so too. He so admired your husband—" Her voice trailed off a moment. "Believe me, if you have a petition that needs signing, I'll sign it. Only I can't leave Ruth here overnight. I always did have respect for your—"

"Ruth Hoving!" Aunt Betty had opened the screen door and was shouting into the house. "Bring Ruth out here! Ruth Hoving!"

"Nothing but respect," the woman mumbled, pulling

a Kleenex from her purse to wipe the sweat from her face. Blue eye shadow was beginning to run, giving her the woebegone look of a circus clown.

"Now, Mrs. Hoving," said Aunt Betty, hands on hips, "we have a boys' dorm on the second floor, a girls' dorm on the third. Do you honestly think I would mix them up?"

"Of course not. Only—"

A girl came out of the house—small, thin, large-eyed, and blonde.

"I didn't know your name was Hoving," Aunt Betty said as if in explanation. "Your mother wants you to go home, Ruth."

The girl looked at her mother. "Mom, I want to stay."

"You're coming home now." She glared at Aunt Betty. "I only let her come in the first place because you needed help. But you have no right to keep my daughter here."

"Thank you for your help, Mrs. Hoving, but I don't need it. And I am not keeping your daughter here."

"Come along, Ruth," the woman said huffily.

"Let me stay one night, Mom. Please?"

"Come along or your father will see to it." Again she glared at Aunt Betty. "My husband doesn't even know she has been here. I did it out of my own good will. And look at the gratitude I get."

Ganesh, watching intently, saw tears well up in the girl's eyes, as she walked over to Aunt Betty and said, "Honest, I'm sorry."

For a moment Aunt Betty hesitated, then smiled and touched the girl's hand. "I appreciate your wanting to help us, Ruth. I won't forget that. But you go on home now."

Slowly the girl left the porch and joined her mother,

who without looking back led her firmly by the elbow down the walk. At the gate Mrs. Hoving said, "I will sign a petition on your behalf!"

Mrs. Hoving turned briskly on her heels and led Ruth away.

Ganesh had never seen his aunt so fiery, so exercised by anything. Her face, suffused by the ruddiness of anger, looked younger. Watching her stride into the yard alone, he followed and in a few minutes joined her.

"Did Mr. Hoving owe Uncle Henry money?" he asked.

Aunt Betty, bending to smell a yellow rose in a flower bed, turned and smiled grimly. "He sure did—and never paid. He was a young mechanic who wanted to start his own garage. Though it would compete with Henry's, Henry wanted to help him out. Now this woman has the audacity to come here and claim she wants to help me! Sign a petition? Respect Henry? That woman and that man? They thought he was weak because he was generous." Aunt Betty cleared her throat to make a declaration. "We are going to fight for this house. Henry lived in this house for years; he loved it too!"

Uncle Henry. And Father. Some people didn't care about handling money with caution, but just the same, they endured in the memory of people who had loved them. Uncle Henry had given his aunt the strength to stand up against Mrs. Hoving. From now on, Ganesh figured, his aunt would not waver in defense of the house. She moved with the power of two.

✖   ✖   ✖

They decided to post nightly guards. It was Tom's idea, since the Satyagraha was in a sense a military operation. Having stood the first duty and then relinquishing the porch to Tom, Ganesh trudged upstairs to his room, which the two boys shared. Through the open window he could hear the rustling of poplars, the ticking of oak limbs against the side of the old house. His house. The house of many people, then and now. Tonight more than a dozen were sleeping within its walls. That was how his great-grandfather had designed the house: to contain many! It was the Indian way with a house too. When he used to stay overnight with Rama, more than a dozen had been there.

Getting up, he walked over to the desk and peered through the moonlight at the elephant-headed god. He did not pray or chant, but reached out and gently touched the bronze figure: Ganesh, the Remover of Obstacles. Was this really happening? Were these American kids helping him defend a house against their own government? Then he lay down and fell quickly to sleep.

×   ×   ×

Tom suggested the next morning that Ganesh hold a Yoga class. Most of the kids wanted to try it, so Ganesh had them fan out on the lawn and taught them some basic positions, standing, sitting, and lying. While he gave instructions, he thought of Tom—not even Rama could have helped him more. Tom had understood that giving Yoga lessons was a way for Ganesh to show his appreciation to the Satyagrahis. A few months ago Ganesh would not have believed such a friend would appear in his new life. He was grateful to Tom, as he surveyed the kids trying Yoga.

After the class, Lucy Smith approached him. "Listen, you better talk to your aunt. She stayed awake all night, sitting on the stairway, to protect us from you boys. We don't need protecting from you guys, okay? We can do our own policing."

Having overheard her angry outburst, Tom Carrington laughed—and laughed harder at Ganesh's confusion and embarrassment. "I guess Indian girls aren't so independent, right?"

Ganesh nodded vigorously. There had been few things harder to adjust to than this easygoing self-reliance in American girls. Back in the village the girls had spoken with quiet restraint, averted their eyes, moved silently in a room almost as if they were not there.

A few minutes later Aunt Betty came onto the porch with a large tray full of paper plates and a serving dish of eggs and bacon. The kids cheered. When she came out the second time, however, bearing the tray with more food, looking puffy-eyed and frazzled from her sleepless night, Lucy Smith stood in her path and spoke sharply. "Mrs. Strepski, we are going to start helping in the kitchen." It was a declaration. "And another thing, Mrs. Strepski. We girls will take care of ourselves."

The eyes of girl and woman met. Then Aunt Betty smiled. "Yes, I guess you can."

This exchange had scarcely ended before someone called out, "Here comes trouble again!"

They all turned to watch the squad car pull up in front of the house. This time, when Chief Halstead got out, he was wearing a gun belt and dark glasses, giving him a more ominous look than on his first visit. At his side was a policeman dressed in the blue gray uniform of the State Police; he was even taller than Chief Halstead and wore a cowboy hat in the style of a Western marshal.

The Satyagrahis stopped eating and put down their paper plates when the policemen reached the invisible wall about ten feet from the porch.

"Good morning, Mrs. Strepski," said Chief Halstead, both men doffing their caps. "This is Officer Baxter of the State Police."

"Good morning, ma'am."

Aunt Betty nodded at them and sat in the rusty swing; it went back and forth, thought Ganesh, with the grating sound of crows outside his window in the village.

Chief Halstead searched for Ganesh, who came forward and took his favorite position on the top step. "Well, Jeffrey, what do you have to say this morning?" the chief said jovially.

"The same as yesterday, sir."

This caused the policeman to frown; he glanced at his companion, as if to say: "This is the kid I told you about."

The State Police officer repeated everything that had been said yesterday about the eviction order. "You," he concluded, looking at Aunt Betty hard, "are in fact now trespassing on state property."

"Sir," began Ganesh, "this is the house where my aunt and father were born. My great-grandfather built it with his own two hands."

The officer ignored Ganesh, keeping his eyes fixed on the woman in the swing. "I think Chief Halstead has given you until noon to vacate. You will be gone then."

"No, sir," said Ganesh from the top step.

The state policeman turned to Chief Halstead. "His name is Jeffrey?"

The chief nodded solemnly.

"Jeffrey," said the state officer, "we have the authority to *carry* you out."

"Carry us out," said Ganesh with a bland smile, "and none of us will be eating."

The state officer smiled too. "Yes, that's what you told Chief Halstead yesterday."

"And still am meaning today." Ganesh moved his legs into the full lotus position, giving himself stability, sending his spine by imagination down, down, down into the earth like an oil drill.

"You're going to a lot of trouble for nothing," the state officer said glumly.

"Not for nothing, sir. You can leave this house and still be having your road, can't you?"

"Tell 'em again what we'll do," whispered Tom, who had seated himself directly behind Ganesh.

"We will eat nothing until the government is listening," said Ganesh. "We will take only water and maybe some bicarbonate of soda. But nothing more." He took a deep decisive breath. "We will start *this noon*."

"What does that mean?" asked Chief Halstead, with a faint but perplexed smile.

"At noon we have our last meal, don't we. No more food until the government is listening."

The officers stared at him a moment, then Chief Halstead stepped forward, hands in his back pockets, studying the kids through his dark glasses.

Suddenly he pointed a thick finger at a small girl. It was Helen Soderstrom, who was a member of the debating team but otherwise rarely spoke. "You," he said. "Will you stop eating like he says?"

Every eye turned to her. Helen had a small mouth, a birthmark on her chin. She didn't weigh a hundred pounds and stood less than five feet. Helen's lips trembled, but in a barely audible voice she said, "Yes, officer."

He thundered, "I can't hear you!"

Her blue eyes blinked rapidly. In a louder voice she said, "Yes, I will!"

For a moment Chief Halstead absorbed that defeat, then walked alongside the porch, studying the faces. "You," he pointed.

"Yes!" another girl affirmed.

"You!"

"Yes!" a boy shouted.

"You!"

"Yes!"

"You!"

"Yes!"

Throwing his arms up in a little gesture of frustration, Chief Halstead did not complete the roll call, but spun on his heel and angrily rejoined the other policeman on the cement walk. They conversed in whispers, then, without another word to the Satyagrahis, returned to the squad car. It moved away from the curb slowly.

✶   ✶   ✶

"Do you mean it, Ganesh?" someone asked him at noon, when everyone congregated for lunch on the porch. "You aren't going to eat after this?"

Ganesh nodded casually, as if agreeing that the weather was good.

"Neither is anybody else going to eat," Tom said.

"Count me out then," declared Ron Merril, who was a plump, ruddy-faced boy. "I will sit here but I won't fast. Not me."

"If you sit," Ganesh said coolly, "you must fast."

"Yeah? Why?"

"Because the government must know we are all deny-

146

ing ourselves. That will show them we are serious."

No one commented for a long while. Then Ron Merril said in a low, exasperated voice, "Okay, I'll give it a try. For a day."

Aunt Betty and two girls emerged from the house carrying paper plates of potato salad and hot dogs. Coming to Ganesh, a girl handed him a plate without hot dogs.

He shook his head. "Please, I will have one of those too."

Everyone stared at him.

Ganesh shrugged. "If you sit with me, I can be eating your food." Soon he looked down at a hot dog steaming on his plate. Slowly, meticulously, cautiously, he cut through it and speared a bite-sized piece of frankfurter on his fork. With the same slow deliberation he lifted it to his mouth.

Then with a little sigh of decision Ganesh opened his mouth and quickly popped the meat in—the first meat he had eaten in his life. For a few moments he didn't chew—dared not—but then taking courage began tentatively to masticate. He forced his jaws to move against the yielding mass. The taste was strong and unappetizing, yet he chewed and chewed and finally, bracing himself and squinting his eyes, swallowed. Sweat broke out on his forehead at the effort it cost him to eat half a hot dog.

"How did you like it?" Tom asked, with his own mouth full of meat.

Ganesh tried to smile, but his discomfort was so obvious that some of the kids giggled in embarrassment.

"You're okay!" a boy exclaimed. It was the one who had angrily questioned Ganesh yesterday about declaring their determination to quit eating.

"After this lunch," Ron Merril said wistfully, "we have nothing but water?"

"And bicarbonate of soda," Ganesh said reassuringly, as if that solved everything.

"Why *that* stuff?" someone asked.

"Gandhi used it when he fasted because it helps settle an empty stomach."

"Didn't Gandhi almost die fasting?" a girl asked.

Ganesh nodded. It was something every Indian knew about their great national leader. "After a while when you fast, you burn up the fat of your body and start consuming protein. My father was telling me that."

"Meaning?"

"You eat up your own body."

There was a long, thoughtful silence. "How long does it take to get to that?" someone else asked.

"That is depending on health and age." Ganesh glanced quickly at his aunt in the swing.

"Don't worry about me," she declared. "I am going to fast. Remember, Jeffrey, you told me Gandhi fasted when he was in his late seventies, so I guess I can do it too."

That afternoon the Satyagrahis continued to lounge on the grass of the yard and play games. Some went inside to watch television. A few boys, including Tom, threw a football around. At intervals throughout the rest of the day, they called home to explain to their parents that they were staying on, at least for another night. No one mentioned the fast. They debated when it would be a good idea to make the fast public. Ganesh sat on the step smiling and listening. He did not tell them that until the fast was public it was of little use. "One thing at a time." His father used to mutter those words when

148

going into the fields to teach farmers about new agricultural methods.

It was during the afternoon that they noticed a few people cruising past the house in slow-moving cars, sticking their heads out of the windows to stare at eleven kids and a middle-aged woman who were defying the law. Public notice began to affect the Satyagrahis. At the outset they had laughed and behaved the way they did during the school recesses; now with a solemn procession of onlookers passing the house, they became quiet, thoughtful. It was what Ganesh wanted. He knew from his father what they did not know: that the success of Satyagraha depended on absolute earnestness, total commitment, and the steadfast ability to suffer. Soon they would understand the consequences of their decision to help him, but not yet. He had eaten meat to become one of them. Now they were going to fast on his behalf. Something very important was beginning to happen between them and him. Ganesh remembered the funeral pyre, approaching it in the procession, his heart beating rapidly, a strange feeling in the pit of his stomach, the hard set of his jaw. It was the same now: he was entering upon something new and difficult, but with the same resolution. As the afternoon waned, he glanced at one after another of the Satyagrahis. He had confronted the funeral pyre on his own, whereas now he had these people of his own age to help him confront a whole government. Never again would he feel lonely in America; not when such people lived here.

✕　　　✕　　　✕

Next morning he held another Yoga class, but only about half participated, the rest admitting they felt sore—

149

even Tom, who limped around the yard like a wounded stork.

Breakfast should have come next, but none came. Faces turned automatically toward the screen door from which Aunt Betty should have emerged with a huge platter of eggs and bacon. But no one said anything until Ron Merril appeared on the porch with his overnight bag slung over his shoulder. Wiping his chubby face with a handkerchief, he admitted that it wasn't possible for him to go without food. He hadn't eaten since yesterday noon—he was starving! And off he went, striding rapidly down the cement walk, bound for home and butter-soaked hotcakes. After Ron had vanished from sight, a few kids began to describe their own hunger symptoms. One said it felt like something crawling inside, another said he felt like throwing up, another felt lightheaded, another had a growling stomach. For all of them, a day had seemed like three or four. Missing one meal wasn't so bad; missing two was still okay. But the worst was waking up in the morning and wanting breakfast, only to discover that the empty feeling would continue for minutes, hours, for the entire day! Someone said it was downright unhealthy. Another said they were still growing and needed more food than most people. What happens to the teeth, someone asked plaintively, if they don't get enough calcium? Would their growth be stunted, their teeth fall out, their legs give way, their hearts stop beating? And how long would all that take? Ganesh, a few grumbled, had hardly been scientific in his estimate: "It depends on health and age." Yeah, but what did that really *mean*?

These bitter and anxious speculations passed among the Satyagrahis while the sun rose into the bright summer air and the tall weather vane, deprived of wind, stood motionless as a piece of cast steel (which it actually was) soldered into the blue sky atop the house.

Ganesh hoped for something to happen soon. For a few days his companions would suffer terribly from hunger pangs—some more than others, but all would feel it more than they had ever expected. To keep their resolution firm and steady, something should happen that would bind them together, making their pain secondary to the commitment they had made.

Fortunately, soon after what could have been lunch time, something did happen.

"Here comes that trouble again!" someone called out, and everyone, as a single body, moved onto the porch and sat down, facing the lawn, up which three men strode briskly after emerging from a black limousine that had pulled up at the curb.

Two of the three men were familiar: Chief Halstead and the State Police officer. But the third wore a checkered business suit and carried a briefcase. Although the police were frowning, the third man smiled all the way up the walk, as if he had good news for everyone. Along with his companions, he stopped at the invisible wall and approached nearer only when Aunt Betty, sitting in the swing, beckoned. "Come, gentlemen, come." The three men edged past the seated kids, both police officers giving Ganesh, who sat on the top step, a long, hard look.

Chief Halstead introduced the man in the checkered suit as State Highway Commissioner Walton. The man grinned before saying, "We have corresponded by mail, but this is the first time I have had the pleasure of meeting you, Mrs. Strepski."

The woman smiled faintly, skeptically at the pretty

speech. "Bring a chair for the commissioner." A boy scooted inside the house and returned quickly with a straight-backed chair.

"Thank you," said Commissioner Walton, whose broad smile seemed fixed on his pleasant, ruddy face. The tall policemen flanked him, as he sat close to the swing. "I would like to explain something, Mrs. Strepski, if you don't mind." He opened the briefcase and hauled out a large hardback notebook. "This contains the proposal and plan of the new highway." In a gentle, persuasive voice, he described the costs involved, the schedule of construction, the estimate of vehicles using the highway annually, the revenue expected from the toll road, the possible uses of such revenue: public service, welfare programs, civil improvements.

Aunt Betty smoothed her old print dress across her lap and said, "I'm glad the state takes an interest in welfare. In his will my husband left a piece of land to this town for the purpose of charity. But this property, the one we are all sitting on, I own myself. When I go, it will be my nephew's."

The commissioner, still smiling, leaned forward to say, "I must point out to you, Mrs. Strepski, what you and your lawyer already know: this property is no longer yours. In fact, we sent you a check in full payment for it according to its present land assessment."

"Which I sent back. I don't want your money. Henry didn't leave me a fortune, far from it, but he provided well enough so I can meet the taxes on my home."

The commissioner, at last, frowned. He glanced around at the kids, who, unlike him, were now smiling. He stared at Ganesh. "Is that him?" he half whispered to Chief Halstead.

"Yes, that's him," said the chief.

"Are you from India, son?" the commissioner asked Ganesh.

"Yes, honored sir."

The euphemism took the man back for a moment, as if he considered the possibility of the boy making fun of him. "So now you're living with your aunt. Well. We are going to provide both of you a nice apartment in town, along with a handsome payment for this house. I suspect the money will see you through college."

Ganesh said nothing.

Nervously the commissioner cleared his throat and turned back to the woman. "Everyone whose property has been appropriated has accepted the fact. Your neighbor, for example." He waved at the land to the left of the house.

"The owner is an absentee landlord who lives in the East," Aunt Betty said disdainfully. "With no stake in this town, in the place he owned here. But what about the hamburger drive-in in the lot next to his? What about appropriating the drive-in?"

"There is a simple explanation, Mrs. Strepski—"

"Because the food chain is holding on to that property with the idea of building something on it later—or selling it at a high price!"

"There is a simple explanation, Mrs. Strepski, which I know you have heard more than once. That property does not lie in the path of the proposed route."

"Then reroute the highway."

She moves with the power of two, thought Ganesh.

The commissioner was now scowling. Briskly he handed the notebook to Aunt Betty. "I urge you to study this. An intelligent woman like yourself will see the good sense

in putting aside private concerns for the public good."
On impulse, it seemed, the commissioner swiveled
around in the chair to look directly at Ganesh. "Well,
son, how do you like America?"

"It is nice, honored sir. But we are not leaving this
house."

The commissioner got to his feet, unable to conceal
his annoyance. "We have no desire to hurt you and your
aunt—" He glanced at the other kids. "Any of you. But
even in America you can't always do as you please. I
understand you have threatened to go on a fast."

"We have begun it, honored sir."

"Then do as you please." Flanked by the policemen
he strode off the porch and turned on the cement walk
to squint in the sunlight at the Satyagrahis. "We won't
carry you off the property. We are not savages. But you
can't fast forever." He gave Aunt Betty a deep frown.
"When you're ready to leave, let us know and we will
put you up in a hotel, Mrs. Strepski." He glanced again
at Ganesh. "You and your nephew."

Everyone watched the three men walk in measured,
self-conscious strides to the limousine and drive off.
When the car had disappeared, someone laughed and
called out to Ganesh, "Hey, you don't call the guy 'honored sir'!"

Tom Carrington bent over and clapped Ganesh on the
shoulder with a big hand. "You're making news. How
did they know you were from India, unless they nosed
around?"

Ganesh, sitting on the top step, smiled, but he was
thinking about something important: the Satyagrahis had
won the first round, because the commissioner maintained they would not be removed bodily from the house.

The authorities did not want to create a fuss by having a bunch of kids carried off someone's property and go home and refuse to eat. So the commissioner and the policemen had decided against the action they originally threatened to take.

Having explained this victory to the others, Ganesh sat back against a porch pillar and wished that Rama were here to share the triumph of a method of protest that had wrested India from British rule.

"So that," murmured Lucy Smith, "is how Satyagraha works."

✕　　✕　　✕

They lived on this success for a day, but it was not enough to satisfy them. Although they pretended that the fast didn't bother them much, it was having an effect, an effect increasing hourly. The Satyagrahis, to allay their pain, played card games with fierce concentration, often quarreling and sometimes forgetting whose turn it was. Others gaped dumbly at television. Some could not sit still for more than a few minutes, but restlessly strolled in the yard, kicking at tufts of grass, pulling leaves from a maple tree, glaring at one another. When the sun went down, they crowded onto the porch and talked, at first aimlessly, mechanically, about anything—about kids and teachers at school, the usual gossip. Then, as night deepened, their nervousness ceased, and they spoke thoughtfully of the future, far more intimately than they had ever done at school or parties. Lucy Smith wanted to be a doctor, Tom Carrington—predictably—a pro basketball player. And then Brad Hoover, a squat, muscular boy with a thick nose, divulged his hidden desire to become a film actor. At school they would have hooted at the idea—short, heavyset Brad—but here, with hunger gnawing at their insides like a rat, none of them laughed. Brad admitted he would be neither tall nor handsome, but not every actor was. Sometimes what counted was the ability to speak lines. Every night at home he recited Shakespeare in front of a mirror. There was a respectful silence until Helen Soderstrom, who wanted to become a teacher, reminded them that the Academy Award had been won once by someone not much taller than Brad.

The Satyagrahis did not stay up late, professing to be tired. Brad took the first guard duty. In the bedroom they shared, Tom fell quickly to sleep, while Ganesh sat up thinking of the day—how slow moving and difficult it had been, like a day in the village when a heat wave sent the temperature above 110 degrees, stunning life into submission while at the same time rattling nerves, shortening tempers.

There was a faint knock at the door. Aunt Betty wanted him to go to her room for a talk.

Once there, she came straight to the point. "I would rather quit, Jeffrey, than see these kids so hungry. The house is not worth it. They try not to show what they feel, but I know. If anyone goes on with the fast, it will be me and me alone."

Wearily Ganesh sat in a chair and looked at his aunt, whose hair was in rollers. "They would never forgive you."

"For letting them live normally again? They wouldn't forgive me for letting them *eat*? Why, I almost screamed looking at them today. Hunger is a horrible thing—horrible."

For a moment Ganesh almost said, "Yes, I have seen

it every day of my life in India." Instead he argued that it would not be fair of her to take away their chance to help. Without waiting for a reply—as if taking for granted that his argument prevailed—Ganesh got up and left the room. Halfway down the hall, he stopped and listened. He had just passed the portrait of his grandfather, who was posed holding a law book at a desk. Had the painting spoken? Of course not. Yet Ganesh had a sense of the old man's presence in the corridor, as if Aunt Betty and his own father were small children skipping along between its two walls, in the heavy wake of a thickset man carrying a huge law book.

✳   ✳   ✳

The next day was very difficult. Hunger peaked; everyone felt snappish, irritable, often at the edge of panic, and they sat and rose and sat again, making the porch their complete space. The old television sat in the parlor, unused. In late morning a boy asked to speak to Ganesh alone, away from the porch, in the yard.

This boy, Ralph Carlson, a member of the wrestling team, hemmed and hawed as he stood with Ganesh near a rose bush. Finally he explained that his parents had phoned and wanted him to come home, because they were leaving town for a while and needed him to go along.

It was clear that the boy wanted to go. And why not? If Ganesh had parents to go somewhere with, perhaps he would have left, perhaps he would have chucked the principles of Satyagraha. He didn't know. He would never know. If he said his commitment was too strong for that, it might be a lie. All he did know was that Ralph Carlson had made a choice, one he must respect. After all, Ralph had given him four days of his life. That was more than some people ever gave anyone.

Impulsively Ganesh reached out and gripped Ralph's muscular arm. "I thank you for coming."

"It isn't that I don't want to stay. I do—" Ralph's voice trailed off in embarrassment. Then, without glancing at the crowd on the porch, he turned and walked out of the yard.

When Ganesh returned to the porch, Lucy Smith frowned at him bitterly. "So Ralph left us," she said.

"He was having to."

"Really?" She gave him an ironic smile. "I happen to know his parents have a cottage on the lake they go to every summer. He was just waiting around for them to call him."

"Here comes someone," Tom called out.

She was a blonde, perhaps in her twenties, wearing slacks and a varicolored blouse, carrying a large shoulder bag. Even without make-up she was pretty. Smiling, she walked through the invisible barrier and placed one foot on the bottom porch step. Leaning forward, she handed a card to Tom Carrington.

Kids crowded around to read it: "Sally Kane. The *Express.*"

"What is the *Express*?" asked Ganesh.

"Biggest newspaper in the state," someone said, looking curiously at the pretty woman.

"I want to meet the boy from India," said Sally Kane with a smile. "That must be you," she pointed at Ganesh, "if you don't know the *Express*." Then she asked him to take a little walk with her in the yard. Ganesh agreed and they strolled past the wilted tulip bed, under a large spreading oak, and stood in the shade.

"This is a nice house," Miss Kane said, appraising the tall clapboard sides, the cast-iron rooster poised above the roof and turning lazily in a gentle breeze. She studied a row of poplars along the left side of the yard, a small vegetable garden in the back.

"It is to me a beautiful house," Ganesh said emphatically.

"You engineered this sit-in, am I right?"

"It is no sit-in, ma'am. It is Satyagraha."

Unslinging the shoulder bag, Miss Kane sat on the ground and patted the grass beside her. "Sit here and tell me about it."

Ganesh did. In the idiom still clinging to his speech from the village, he explained that Satyagraha is not passive resistance or weakness, but direct action, the purpose being to confront an opponent with the demand that he make a choice. It is a means of achieving agreement by assuming that your oppressor can change over to your way of thinking. Another basic assumption is that you too learn, by examining your own motives, whether they are worthwhile or not. Ultimately Satyagraha ends in mutual liberation.

Ganesh concluded, "That is what we are doing. Like that."

Miss Kane put down the pad on which she was writing. "Who taught you this?"

"My father. But most Indians are knowing it."

"A lot of people have criticized Gandhi. They say he was too idealistic."

Ganesh shrugged.

"Doesn't their criticism matter to you?"

"Not for the house."

"What makes this Satyagraha actually work?"

"Self-control," Ganesh replied without hesitation.

"You think you have that?"

Ganesh nodded.

"And so now you and those other kids are on a serious fast. It *is* serious, isn't it?"

"Yes, ma'am. We take only water."

"How did you convince them to undergo such a thing?"

"I told them the house was all my aunt and I were having in the world. And they believed."

The reporter stared thoughtfully at the freckle-faced boy. "Well, Jeffrey Moore, in my opinion you don't stand a chance. Yet the word is out around the capital. You've been heard sufficiently for my paper to send me down here for an interview. So—who knows?" The young woman got to her feet and stared at the other kids lolling on the porch. "A fast is painful, isn't it, Jeffrey."

"Yes, ma'am."

"Your aunt is fasting too?" she added. "It could be dangerous for her."

"She will be doing it anyway."

"Aren't you concerned for her welfare?"

"Yes, ma'am, I am," Ganesh said quietly.

The woman reporter studied him a long time: his blond hair, his light blue eyes, his freckles. "Good luck," she said finally. "Good luck, Jeffrey Moore—and I mean it."

✕   ✕   ✕

Throughout the rest of the day people strolled past the gate, some leaning on the fence to squint curiously at the fasters. There were two camps among the spectators: those for and those against Mrs. Strepski, her Indian nephew, and the town kids helping them. Some people figured they were a bunch of lawbreakers having summer fun. Others thought it was unfair to destroy such a lovely house, one of the oldest in town. And for what? For a sheet of concrete on which motorists would have new opportunities for killing one another. Some people thought of the additional cost of changing blueprints and initiating a new purchase of land. Others felt the state had been highhanded in dealing with the rights of ordinary citizens, and it was time to put a stop to such dictatorial practices. So the controversy continued along the length of the white picket fence until darkness set in; even then a parade of cars, idling slowly down the street, let the fasters know that the town was now fully aware of Satyagraha.

That evening, about the time there should have been dinner, Culver Williamson abruptly turned belligerent. He was a popular boy, a fine athlete, a good student whose sudden outburst surprised everyone. He yelled through the humid darkness at Ganesh.

"This is crazy! What in hell am I *doing* here? *Tell me!*"

When Ganesh did not reply, Culver repeated the question angrily. "Come on, tell me! What is this? I'm sitting here hour after hour unable to think of anything but food. For *what?*"

"Because you are thinking it is worthwhile," Ganesh said coolly.

"Worthwhile?" Culver snorted in derision. "What's worthwhile about sitting on the porch of an old house waiting to get so hungry we all go home—and the house is torn down? It doesn't make sense. Who decided we would do it? *You?*"

"If you are not deciding for yourself, you must leave."

Culver was silent a few moments, absorbing those

blunt words. Then in the faint starlight he addressed all of the fasters. "I don't know how the rest feel, but with me it was an adventure at the start. Right?"

Others murmured in agreement.

"But it's not anymore."

"Yeah," someone said. "Right. It sure isn't."

"Then what *is* it?"

No one, not even Ganesh, answered. In a little while, one by one, the Satyagrahis left the porch for their rooms.

"Culver," said Ganesh, rising. "You are having the first guard duty."

At one o'clock in the morning, Culver came upstairs and woke Tom to take the next shift.

Ganesh was awake, listening.

"Are you okay?" Tom asked in a nervous whisper.

"Sure I'm okay," said Culver. "Why shouldn't I be?"

"I think everyone was glad you asked those questions," said Tom.

"You think so?" Culver sounded relieved.

"They were questions everyone wanted to ask."

"Nobody thought I was a quitter or anything?"

"Nobody," Tom assured him.

"Because when you come down to it," Culver announced tensely, "I bet I would be one of the last to leave."

Ganesh closed his eyes and sighed, finally able to sleep.

✖   ✖   ✖

During the next day there were more communications with parents, who realized that the "adventure at the Strepski house" was lasting longer than they had anticipated. Either they called or came up the front lawn with questions. Are you all right? Are you eating well? (A question the Satyagrahis evaded, since they had agreed not to divulge the fast until it was so firmly established they could not give it up.) Are you having a good time? Have the authorities bothered you? So this is Ganesh! Hello, Ganesh.

But secrecy about the fast ended that afternoon, when a neighbor brought over to the house the latest edition of the *Express*. Everyone crowded around to read the story, which appeared on the front page under the caption:

YOUNG PEOPLE DEFEND HOUSE

The first part of the article was a factual account of the situation. The following lines ended the article:

> It is the first such incident in this state since the 1960 sit-ins at the university. One of the young defenders objected to the term "sit-in," because of its connotation of willful rebellion. Instead, he called it a method of arriving at a true state of affairs. The idea is to appeal to the conscience of people in power. But late yesterday State Highway Commissioner Walton reaffirmed the government's legal right to take possession of the Strepski property and suggested that steps are being taken to assert that right. The governor was not available for comment on the matter.
>
> Meanwhile, the youthful defenders have vowed to fast until the authorities have a change of heart. The youngsters are now into their fifth day of a severe fast, taking nothing but plain water.

The last paragraph had the parents hurrying to the house or calling anxiously on the phone. It was okay to sit on a porch,. but they didn't want the health of their children tampered with. Yet each parent faced silence and determination; the Satyagrahis had put five whole days of suffering into this house and therefore their commitment was formidable, unlike anything their parents had expected from them. Only one Satyagrahi was persuaded to leave—an underweight boy with a history of illness. He left, however, only when the other kids joined his parents in urging him to go. Ganesh assured him that every day, morning and night, they would phone him and offer a detailed account of what was happening. This promise counted more with the boy than all the pleading. So he got his overnight bag and left— but slowly. Almost every step down the cement walk, he turned and waved at his companions, with his parents silent and humble, matching his dilatory pace all the way to their car.

That day the fasters felt more weak than hungry. They slept a lot of the time, passing quickly from a lazy consciousness into a deep sleep. They curled up on the floorboards of the porch and let the hours flow past them like currents of hot summer air. They stopped playing cards and rarely talked. Sluggish and drowsy, they paid no attention to the growing crowd of spectators, who had been brought to the house by the *Express* story. A squad car patrolled the street regularly to discourage any sort of disturbance.

That evening the fasters moved out of the dorms and slept on blankets piled on the porch—all except Aunt Betty, who trudged weakly to her bedroom.

It was a hot, humid night, one that reminded Ganesh

of the village, of his talks with Father under the peepul tree, when even the slightest motion would make them break out in a sweat. On such a night the two worlds—American town and Indian village—seemed to merge for him; with the Satyagrahis near him, there was no chance of feeling lonely or alien. Crickets bleeping in the undergrowth added to his sense of oneness; that familiar sound had been with him throughout his life. Each night in the tiny village house the chorus of crickets erected a great wall of sound and now here in this house a similar wall rose into the darkness, telling him the world was one.

The next day followed the same monotonous pattern. Hunger proved less troublesome, but in its stead was a paralyzing sense of fatigue. The Satyagrahis lounged on the porch like cows and goats seeking shade in the heat of an Indian afternoon. As they leaned against the porch wall or curled up or lay outstretched on their backs, Ganesh recalled the stunned life of the village when summer heat crept into the bloodstream, slowing it down, immobilizing every muscle, until only lizards and birds thrived in the sweltering glare. His father had once told him of the tricks a fast could play on the mind and body, but there was a vast difference between hearing about it and experiencing it. How did these American kids do so well? Ganesh at least knew how to meditate and calm his mind, so he could stand against the momentary panic threatening his resolution. But somehow his companions matched his own will. It occurred to Ganesh that even with meditation he might not hold out unless they were with him. Maybe that's why they could all go through with it—they moved with communal power.

Yet the fast did not go smoothly. That evening Brad

Hoover suddenly maintained the fast would not work. It was going to fail because the authorities had only to sit back and wait. "They can watch us starve to death."

"Ah, they wouldn't do that," argued Tom Carrington, but in a voice lacking conviction.

"Sitting here," continued Brad, "I imagined we were all stretched out on the porch, and the cops and a lot of other people were stepping among us, inspecting the bodies for signs of life, and someone was saying, 'They went too far, these kids did, they went past the point of no return!'"

"I don't think I'm hungry," Helen Soderstrom remarked after a long silence. "No, I'm not hungry. What does it mean when you're not hungry anymore? Are you—dying?"

"After a while, you are losing hunger," Ganesh explained. "We should all be feeling better soon."

"How do you know?"

"My father told me. Once my father fasted for twenty-one days when he was with Swamiji."

"Was he okay?"

"No," Ganesh said candidly. "He developed a kidney problem. It took him a long time to be getting his health back." Ganesh added, "But that was a long fast."

"How long is this one going to be?" someone asked in the shadows.

Ganesh did not answer. An unasked question hovered in the steamy night air: will we fall sick too?

❋   ❋   ❋

Ganesh's prediction came true: the next day they all felt better. They experienced a resurgence of energy and total freedom from hunger pangs and from fatigue too.

They strolled in the yard, staring in wonder at flowers and blades of grass, as if seeing everything for the first time.

Ganesh nodded when they told them how wonderful they felt. "It is like burning away what was not good inside. You are feeling light, free. Father told me. Like that."

"Yeah, but then he fell sick," someone reminded Ganesh.

About noon the sky clouded over, bringing into the yard a watery gray light that enhanced the greenness of leaf and grass. Then a faint but steady rain began to fall, pinning the Satyagrahis to the porch. Everyone crowded together against the house, as the rain fell musically, lending a sparkle to the cement of the front walk.

None of the Satyagrahis felt like sleeping; with their new-found energy they became restless, imprisoned within the rectangle of the porch by the pelting rain.

Tom Carrington abruptly exclaimed that this was the worst of all.

Everyone stared at him.

"Having nothing to do for so long," he explained. "Just sitting here. I'm not used to it."

"Me either!" others agreed.

They all stared at the rain, so gripped by communal power that they could not go inside the house, but had to remain on the porch, jailed by gray bars of rain.

"There is a way not to be restless," Ganesh declared.

Someone laughed. "Another Indian idea?"

He nodded emphatically. "You can meditate and calm the mind."

"What's so good about doing that?"

"The mind is a monkey," Ganesh said. "Always in

motion. Stop it from moving, you are not feeling restless."

"And then?"

Ganesh paused a moment, considering the answer. It occurred to him suddenly, in a flash of insight, that meditation was an experience similar to that he had on the Cauvery River. He said, "You feel a part of everything. You are here and everywhere. We are all here and everywhere."

No one spoke.

Then he added, with a sigh, "Anyway, meditation is the hardest thing you might ever be trying in your life."

"Can you do it?" someone asked.

"Only a little," Ganesh admitted.

"How do you start?"

Ganesh sat in the lotus position—legs crossed with heels on opposite thighs—with the palms of his hands upward in his lap. "Now close your eyes," he said.

"Is that all?"

Ganesh laughed. "It might be seeming that way. Only it is hard."

"How come?"

"Try it."

So they all did. Not all of them could sit in the lotus position, as it required a great deal of suppleness. They sat therefore with only one heel on the opposite thigh in the half-lotus position. They put their hands, palms upward, in their laps, closed their eyes, and—meditated. Within a couple of minutes someone giggled, then most of them did. All of them opened their eyes and looked around in amusement.

"I see what you mean," Tom said sheepishly. "You close your eyes and your mind keeps going!"

"Like a monkey in a cage," Ganesh said with a smile.

"So how do you calm it down?"

Ganesh explained there was more than one way. You might repeat a mantra again and again—hundreds of times without stopping. Or you might ask yourself continually a question: Who am I? And another question: Who is asking who am I? And pursue those two questions like a hunter. Or you could have an image of someone you love or worship in your mind and focus upon it constantly.

"Like the face of Jesus?" asked Helen Soderstrom.

Ganesh nodded. He did not tell her that, in his village, people who meditated used the face of Shiva, Vishnu, or Shakti.

Lucy Smith asked, "What method do you use?"

"I am watching my breath."

A few Satyagrahis laughed at the idea.

"Yes, I am trying it," Ganesh affirmed. "You sit with eyes closed and think you see your breathing coming into your nose, then going down into your whole body, then leaving through the nose. You see it coming in and going out, coming in and going out, and you do nothing else but that—just see it. And when your mind is playing the monkey again, you bring it back to the breath, always to the breath."

Someone asked did it really work.

"For me a little," Ganesh said. "But with time it will be working a lot for anybody. Like that. With much, much practice. Until it is not necessary to watch the breath, but the mind is steady, like the light of the sun. Try again."

So they did, each in his own way, but the experiment lasted scarcely five minutes before the giggling started again and they were talking about what had happened during those few short minutes. Ganesh listened, and it seemed to him that he was listening to himself in the house of his Yoga Master, making the same discoveries, having the same trouble with the mind as they were having. The awareness for him in the village was the awareness for them on the porch: concentration broken by the sound of rain or by a fly crawling on the skin or by a worry or a memory or a self-conscious realization that this was an attempt at calming the mind.

Still, in the village, among his companions and guided by his guru, he had learned patience, far more, he suspected, than his fellow Satyagrahis had at their command. Or so he thought until that evening. It was during a stroll after the rain had stopped. Culver Williamson came up alongside him in the wet grass.

"About that meditation," Culver began in a hushed tone, as if afraid someone might overhear. "For a while— I mean I think so—my mind was calm. I mean, it stopped thinking about everything. It just watched my breath. At least I think it happened."

"How did you feel?"

"It was not like anything else." He added, "And so good I didn't want it to stop. But it did."

"Then it really happened," said Ganesh, recalling how his guru had once told him the same thing. He reached out and touched Culver's muscular arm, unable to explain to the athlete that he had just achieved something as difficult as anything he had ever accomplished on the football field.

✗ ✗ ✗

Next morning, one by one, the Satyagrahis trudged upstairs to take showers—their daily substitute for breakfast—and then returned to the porch, which otherwise they never left. In fact, they occupied only the middle and western portions, leaving the east side empty, as they crowded together like guests at the Mad Hatter's tea party.

Lucy Smith, seeing Ganesh leave the porch to walk down to the mailbox, got up and accompanied him. "I'm worried about Helen," she said on the way. "Her hands are shaking."

"Did you ask her how she is feeling?"

"That's what really worries me. Helen said she felt good and gave me such a look—"

"If she is sick, she must be stopping."

"I don't think we can stop her."

"We can be calling her parents."

"We do and she won't ever speak to us again. I know Helen."

Ganesh stopped and looked at the pretty girl. "Is it true?"

"Helen is small and doesn't look strong, but I wouldn't want to stand in her way."

Ganesh stared down at the cement walk. Father had told him if he didn't understand what to do in a situation, he had better wait and see.

"What shall we do?" asked Lucy. "Wait and see?"

Ganesh could not help but smile. "That is a good idea," he said. "We will be doing like that."

Then he walked to the mailbox and withdrew a magazine and one letter—from India, from Rama!

Don't read it now, Ganesh told himself abruptly. He didn't know why, but something told him to save the letter to read at another time. When? He didn't know. But he must keep it awhile.

No sooner had he and Lucy returned to the porch than a fat elderly man waddled up the cement walk, wiping his bald sweaty head with a handkerchief. "Is Mrs. Strepski in?" he asked. "Tell her Mr. Patton has come."

In a few minutes Aunt Betty appeared on the porch, looking pale and weary. She walked unsteadily to the swing and sat down. "Good morning, Bruce," she said in a small voice. "Come sit down."

"No, Betty, I'm rushed today." He stood at the bottom step, regarding her critically. "You don't look well."

"I feel just fine."

"Oh, sure. It's the fasting, isn't it." He glanced reproachfully at the kids ranged to one side of the porch. "Last night I had a call from Commissioner Walton."

"So now he's calling my lawyer!" Aunt Betty exclaimed in surprise. "Is he going to listen to reason?"

"Not any reason you want him to listen to, Betty," said Mr. Patton. "He was damn angry at you giving interviews to the press."

"I'm glad the *Express* saw fit to send a reporter. We got some good publicity out of it. It will move public opinion."

"All it did was move Walton to anger. Now give me a moment, Betty," said the lawyer, his voice turning buttery and persuasive. "You simply must not go on with this thing. It won't work, there is no chance at all. Walton convinced me of that. Why didn't you consult me first? And at your age—fasting!"

"Gandhi did it."

"Sure, but he was a little Indian fellow—" His last remark apparently made Mr. Patton think of her nephew. "Which one is Jeffrey?" he asked, turning to the kids. "Well, shall we go inside and talk there?" he added.

"No," she said. "Whatever you have to say can be said in front of my friends."

"Oh—your friends," he repeated condescendingly. He glanced at the Satyagrahis. "If that's the way you want it."

"It is."

"Commissioner Walton assures me they have made definite arrangements for you to have a two-bedroom apartment in the new building on Vine and Second. You know. The one that just started renting?"

"I know."

Mr. Patton chuckled with forced heartiness. "People are *clamoring* for rentals there! But it's all been arranged for you and—" He looked around, seeking her resemblance among the frowning youngsters. "And your nephew."

Without hesitation Aunt Betty said, "Tell Walton I am obliged. Also tell him, if he is really concerned with my welfare, to buy the hamburger stand from that big food chain and let me keep my house."

She moves with the power of two, thought Ganesh.

"Is that your decision?" Mr. Patton asked stiffly.

"It is."

"As your attorney I strongly advise you to take Walton's offer. You can't win this battle—even with *their* help." He turned toward the kids and glared at them. "All you are doing now is alienating the officials who are willing to help you—and ruining your health; that is plain! Do I have your final word?"

"Yes, Bruce, you do."

A spontaneous cheer went up from the Satyagrahis as the fat man huffed his way down the sunny cement walk.

*　　*　　*

That night, a moonlit one, Ganesh sat up against the porch railing, his feet straight out, staring at his sleeping companions. Moments earlier he had awakened from a deep sleep, coming to attention like an animal suddenly alert to danger. Now, breathing easy, he studied the huddled forms of the Satyagrahis. Ganesh had nothing but admiration for them. The house might have been their own, considering their intense commitment to its defense.

Moonlight. It streamed through the porch railings, striping the floorboards. Moonlight. How often he had sat with his father under the peepul tree in moonlight! During most of Father's last illness, he suddenly realized, the nights had been moonlit. In moonlight he had listened to his father trying to distill the experience of a lifetime. But one thing Father had not mentioned was the beauty of friendship. Why? Ganesh asked that now. Why? Perhaps because Father had remained an alien in his adopted land. In truth, Father had been alone, shoring up his new life and new beliefs without help from the past, and when Mother was gone, there had been no one to help him in the present. Swami had not been a real friend; he and Father had shared a different sort of experience. They had yearned together for God, but without having felt for each other what Ganesh now felt for his American companions and they for him. Ganesh had discovered friendship for himself. His father's wisdom had not touched upon it, so it had been his own truth to find and cherish. Moonlight slanted across the heads of his sleeping friends, a ghostly wash of silver, a silent ocean in which he hoped they swam gently through good

174

dreams. Ganesh looked up at the roof of the porch, aware that beyond it were two floors of the house and a peaked roof, above which stood a cast-iron rooster dominating the entire yard. This house, rising above him, contained many spirits, both living and dead. Ganesh closed his eyes. He did not count his breath or repeat a mantra, but let his consciousness free itself and drift lightly among the spirits—those of his ancestors, his parents, those of his aunt, his loyal friends. The house was peopled by past and present.

× × ×

Next day many people stood outside the gate not long after sunrise. Most of them, by the look of their overalls and cheap cotton dresses and beet-red faces, were farmers. A stocky woman with very fat legs trudged up the walk bearing a large bouquet of flowers. Satyagrahis got Aunt Betty out to the porch in a hurry. By the time she arrived, the heavyset woman had been standing patiently near the front steps, gripping the bouquet in a rough, stubby hand.

"How d'ya do," the woman said and thrust the flowers forward.

Lucy Smith dashed down the steps, took the bouquet with a smile, and handed it to Aunt Betty, who slumped wearily in the swing.

"Thank you," Aunt Betty murmured. Smelling the flowers she added, "You are very kind."

"My husband and me just wanted you to know we don't like what the state is doing. Land is land. When you live on it, you own it; it's yours, no matter what a judge says. Leastwise that is what we was taught and live by. So we want you to know God Bless You, and we wish you luck." Without awaiting a reply, the plump woman turned and was gone.

"That's a good sign," remarked Lucy Smith when the woman had waddled out of sight. "It means people know what we're doing and why."

"You see," Tom explained to Ganesh, "this is a farm state. The politicians pay attention to what the farmer thinks."

Ganesh understood farmers from his own experience. All his life he had seen them bending in the fields, tracking through mud churned by oxen, lying exhausted in bullock carts taking burlap bags full of rice to market. He knew how much a farmer loved and respected the land. "Yes," he said to Lucy and Tom, "it's a good sign."

The day, though beginning on a hopeful note, did not continue that way. Euphoria disappeared and a general weakness returned. The Satyagrahis grew both restless and lethargic, bored, yet too fatigued for any activity. Hour followed remorseless hour. The Satyagrahis edged closer together in their increasing depression, in their need for sharing the worst experience of all—this new terrible emptiness. Some tried to meditate, but soon gave it up. Even Ganesh failed at it. Not that he was surprised; Father had told him how tricky meditation could be, how it might go well and then suddenly deceive you, making you feel worse than you had before attempting it.

Something peculiar and disturbing occurred during the heat of afternoon. They were all on the porch (except Aunt Betty, who rarely left her bedroom now), when suddenly Helen Soderstrom began sobbing. People gathered around, trying to soothe her, but she shrugged them off as if they were enemies.

"Go away, go away!" she sobbed, curling up in a ball against the side of the porch. "I love this house," she murmured. Then in a louder voice she exclaimed again, "I love this house! I love this house!" Falling abruptly silent, she sniffled a few times and stared at the wall.

It was at this moment that Ganesh took the folded unread letter from his back pocket. He must break the spell of her despair, of the despair as yet concealed in the hearts of everyone.

"Listen," he said, opening the envelope. "This is a letter from my friend in the village." He read slowly, while in nearby trees a few sparrows chirped and flies buzzed through the spacious avenue of the open porch.

"Dear Ganesh, I was very glad to be having news from you, knowing you are in good health. My family sends best regards too. The hot season is finished, and we are having a breeze in the evenings. Subramanian broke his leg last week jumping from a hay mound. He was not aware that underneath the paddy hay was a big sharp stone. Vasu and I went viper hunting yesterday but caught only one. He does not have your eyes. Remember how we would be going through a field and you would be stopping like that and whisper 'there,' and I would look hard but see nothing and then when we took one step more, the viper would dart out through the grass?

"We miss you, all of us. We had such good times, you and me especially. I won't let you forget the village and all of us here. But I can tell from your letter that you are making such good friends and that makes me happy too. The other day Subish—Subish from the crematory—stopped me and asked to be remembered to you. So you see, you have friends in both places. The other night I had a dream and in it you were coming toward me with people I didn't know, all of you smiling. That was a good dream, wasn't it. Write. Your friend, Rama."

"He sounds okay," someone murmured.

Helen Soderstrom was sitting up.

✖   ✖   ✖

When night fell, they huddled even closer together. Someone asked in the darkness, "How long have we been here?"

Nobody answered right away.

"Didn't we keep track?" There was giggling.

"We have now fasted eleven days," Ganesh informed them.

A low awed whistle went through the night air.

"Ganesh! Come here!" Lucy Smith stood in the doorway holding the screen door open.

When Ganesh joined her, Lucy said nervously, "Your aunt isn't well."

They went upstairs; Aunt Betty lay in her bedroom panting, lips drawn, her face not haggard but—bloated.

Ganesh sat down on the bed and took her hand. It was feverish. "Aunt, you must have a doctor."

"Don't you dare stop me now," she said feebly, her eyes fierce, as she lifted her head from the pillow.

"You must be having a doctor, ma'am. Or we quit."

Aunt Betty glared at him. "You'd go this far and *quit*? I don't believe it of you; I refuse to believe it of you!" Her lips were tense, straight in determination. "You must never quit!"

"We won't," Lucy Smith put in suddenly and stepped up to the bed. "Your nephew is wrong. We won't quit,

178

any of us. If he does, then we'll stay without him." She glared at Ganesh as his aunt had done.

Aunt Betty smiled wanly. "I believe you. All right, call the doctor."

In a half-hour her physician was in the bedroom, examining her, while Ganesh and the other Satyagrahis waited in the hall. The doctor, a white-haired, bent old man, finally emerged with his medical bag. "So you're the nephew," he said to Ganesh severely. "I must say, you and your friends have got your aunt into a real pickle." He put up one hand to discourage interruption. "Nothing serious—yet. It's a kidney problem. Develops with some people during a fast. Right now I can control it, but if she persists in this folly—" He shrugged and scowled. "It could get worse."

"How much worse?" asked Ganesh.

"It could become fatal."

Ganesh swallowed hard. "When could it be getting like that?"

"Who can say? In a matter of this sort it depends on a lot of factors. Each body is unique in a fast. Maybe five days, maybe two—maybe tomorrow." The doctor gripped Ganesh's shoulder with a clawlike hand. "Convince her she must stop."

"She won't."

With a sigh of exasperation the doctor said briskly, "I can only advise, I can't command." He left the Satyagrahis standing in the hall.

"We better quit," someone said.

"No!" chorused the others.

"Never," Culver Williamson muttered between his teeth.

Ganesh stared at them a moment, then went into the bedroom.

Aunt Betty waved her hand weakly. "I'm okay," she claimed with a faint smile.

"What good is this house," Ganesh said, tears in his eyes, "if something happens to you?"

"What good is it? It's everything. It just isn't a house, Jeffrey," she said, patting the bed lightly for him to sit beside her. "It means you and they—" She pointed toward the door, behind which the Satyagrahis were waiting. "You must stand up for your beliefs. Those friends of ours out there are in it as deeply as we are. You can't let them down any more than I can."

"If anything happens to you," Ganesh said in a low voice, "I would be hating this house."

"Then hate it. But you must fight for it anyway."

She moves with the power of two, thought Ganesh.

"Do you understand me?" she asked sharply.

"No."

"You started with—what did you call it?—a firm grip on the truth. Do you still have that grip?"

"Yes, ma'am, I do."

"Enough said, then. Go out and let me rest." She took his hand and squeezed it, adding, "Don't you give up for *anything*. Hear?"

Nodding, he withdrew his hand and went into the hall. The others had all gone downstairs. When he reached the porch, there was silence. Ganesh sat down with his back against the wall, staring into the moonlight. No one said a word, because words were no longer necessary.

A few minutes later the phone rang. Lucy Smith

came to the screen door and called into the darkness of the porch for Ganesh, who rose and went inside the house.

When he said hello into the phone, from the other end came a soft, pleasant voice: "This is Sally Kane. From the *Express.* Remember?"

"We thank you for the news report," Ganesh told her.

"I suspect you're in for a lot more publicity. That's why I'm calling. A friend of mine says a TV unit is coming to your house tomorrow for an interview. Do you understand what that means?"

Ganesh, still overwhelmed by what was happening to his aunt, said nothing.

"It means," continued Sally Kane, "the state is going to be *very* interested in your problem. TV isn't exactly what the officials want. TV could have a big influence on their decision." She paused. "Is something wrong?"

"Yes, my aunt is sick."

"I see. Because of the fast. Well, what are you going to do?"

"Continue."

"She wants that?"

"She is wanting it. We all are."

"Including you?"

After a long pause, Ganesh said faintly, "Yes. I too."

"Then good luck. I know it isn't easy—"

"Thank you, Miss Kane. It is not." After hanging up, he went to the porch and told everyone about the TV. No one shouted hurrah; no one said a thing, but, like Ganesh, sat there grimly determined. Nothing was going to change their mind, nothing good or bad. They were sitting until the house was free.

✖   ✖   ✖

He awoke in the darkness with a violent start. The moon had gone past the porch, leaving the sky studded with brilliant little points of starlight. Had he been dreaming? Had it been a nightmare? Something had shaken him, perhaps the fear of his aunt dying. It was all very well to believe in something to the exclusion of other things. But at what cost might he be defending this house? He could not lose his aunt so soon after finding her. Ganesh stirred, feeling compelled to rise and tiptoe past the sleeping bodies to the screen door, then up the stairway to his own room.

From this side of the house the moonlight was shining through the window upon the bronze figure on the desk. At this moment Ganesh understood that it was the elephant-headed god who had compelled him to come upstairs. He reached down and picked it up, hefting it to sense its bronze weight, peering closely at the tiny eyes, the curved trunk, the huge ears, the great belly, the four arms. In America it had sometimes seemed an odd, perhaps ridiculous object, unrelated to the image that had been worshiped during his life in the village. Yet often in the past Ganesh had been comforted by it, and once again, as he had during his father's illness, he desperately needed comfort. Replacing the bronze figure on the desk, Ganesh dropped on his knees before it. He no longer worried if it was really a symbol of God or if it had any power or if in the past it had ignored or betrayed him. The elephant-headed god was right here, a vision conjured in the minds of countless people for centuries, in great temples, in wayside shrines, in little puja rooms inside modest homes, on calendars, in souvenir stalls during festival times. People believed in it, whatever it was, however capable it was of helping them in their distress. There was nothing wrong in such a belief. Nothing. Ganesh lifted his hands in prayer and recited a mantra to his namesake god. He did it with feeling, without embarrassment, simply repeating the gestures and words of men, women, and children from time beyond reckoning. Satisfied, he rose and went away. Back on the porch, he lay on his side and stared at the faint outline of the white picket fence until falling asleep.

✕   ✕   ✕

He heard something stirring nearby and opened his eyes to look into those of Lucy Smith, also lying on the floorboards of the porch. They both smiled and sat up. Others were waking too in the gray mist of morning. A ground fog undulated like ocean waves on top of the grass, a freshness of air stimulated the wakers, who stretched, yawned, and blinked.

Ganesh went immediately upstairs to check on his aunt, who slept quietly, her face relaxed, her breathing slow and regular. He would let her sleep as long as she could.

Coming back downstairs, he opened the screen door in time to see, along with everyone else on the porch, a black limousine pull up to the curb.

Emerging from it was the man in the checkered suit, carrying the familiar briefcase: Commissioner Walton. This time he was not accompanied by the police, but walked unattended up the walk, with fog ballooning around his knees at every step. Reaching the invisible barrier, he stopped and gravely studied the people gathered on the porch. He asked for Mrs. Strepski.

Ganesh stepped forward and explained that his aunt was sleeping.

"I understand she is not well," Commissioner Walton remarked. "Her doctor called me." He frowned deeply at Ganesh, as if he had given the freckle-faced boy a lot of thought recently. "You have caused her—you have caused *all* your friends a lot of trouble," he said.

"Yes, sir," Ganesh admitted quietly. "I know it. Like that."

"But in the face of it you will have the fast continue?"

"Yes, sir."

Commissioner Walton cleared his throat. "Well, that won't be necessary." He explained in crisp sentences, as if the saying of each one pained him, that at an extraordinary session of the Highway Commission Planning Board last night a change had been proposed in the plan. In the light of public interest, the board was going to reroute the highway by confiscating the drive-in and restoring the property of Mrs. Strepski under the legal designation of a Landmark Building, safeguarded by a statute related to the State Historical Society.

Commissioner Walton stared gloomily at the assembled kids. "I wanted you to know," he told Ganesh, "as soon as possible, so your aunt will stop this fasting and let the state get back to its regular business!" Turning on his heel, he charged through the flowing mist.

The Satyagrahis watched the big black car vanish through the early morning like smoke.

"Shouldn't we give a cheer or something?" Tom Carrington suggested, but instead of initiating it, he sat down against the house and put his hands in his pockets. No one else took up his idea, but everyone else sat down too.

"We'll cook breakfast pretty soon," Lucy Smith maintained, but curiously without enthusiasm, as if she were unwilling to see the end of their trial. "Ganesh," she said, "is it all right if I give the news to your aunt?"

"No one else should," Ganesh said, remembering how last night she had stood against him, against the world, in defense of the house. When Lucy had gone inside, he walked into the dewy grass through oceanic layers of fog. They had won, but for a while the thrill of victory was eluding them. It would come soon. But in those few moments before the Satyagrahis took hold of their triumph, he had the silence of the morning to himself. He walked away from the house to view it from the yard. Midway between it and the picket fence, Ganesh turned and stared through the mist at the weather vane, at the cast-iron rooster fixed securely above the house long ago by his great-grandfather to signify for everyone that here was a place of shelter, a home of memory.